DISAPPEARANCE AT HANGMAN'S BLUFF

A FELONY BAY MYSTERY

J. E. Thompson

WALDEN POND PRESS

An Imprint of HarperCollins*Publishers*

Walden Pond Press is an imprint of HarperCollins Publishers.
Walden Pond Press and the skipping stone logo are trademarks
and registered trademarks of Walden Media, LLC.

Library of Congress Cataloging-in-Publication Data
Thompson, J. E.
    Disappearance at Hangman's Bluff : a Felony Bay mystery / J. E.
Thompson. — First edition.
        pages   cm
    Summary: "When Abbey and Bee's neighbor's dog, Yemassee, is
kidnapped, they decide it's their job to find the men who took him"—
Provided by publisher.
    ISBN 978-0-06-210449-6 (hardcover)
    [1. Mystery and detective stories. 2. Robbers and outlaws—
Fiction. 3. Best friends—Fiction. 4. Friendship—Fiction. 5. Charleston
(S.C.)—Fiction.]   I. Title.
PZ7.T3715957Dis 2014   2014001882
[Fic]—dc23   CIP
                                                                 AC

Typography by Alicia Mikles
14 15 16 17 18   CG/RRDH   10 9 8 7 6 5 4 3 2 1
❖
First Edition

To Ella, Hadley, Will, and James,

my next generation of readers

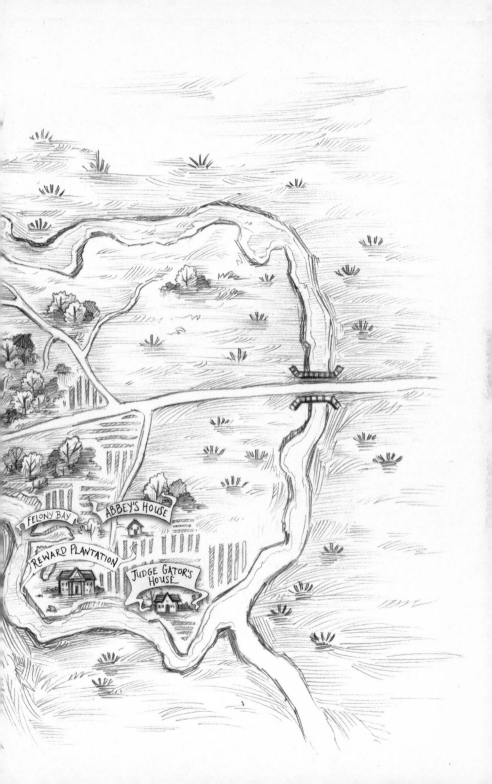

FELONY BAY

ABBEY'S HOUSE

REWARD PLANTATION

JUDGE GATOR'S HOUSE

One

If you hurt a horse, puppy, dog, or pony, I will hurt you back. I am only a twelve-year-old girl, but I will hurt you really, really bad. That's a promise.

Now that we have that straight, I should introduce myself. My name is Abbey Force. My best friend is Bee Force. We share the same last name, but we're not sisters. We aren't even cousins, and we certainly don't act the same. Long story short, I am usually the one who gets us into trouble, and Bee is almost always the one who gets us out of it.

My real name isn't Abbey. It's Abigail, but my teachers and my father are the only ones who can get away with calling me that, and even they do it only when I'm in trouble. Anybody else, if they don't want a bloody nose, calls me Abbey. In case you don't get it, I *hate* the name Abigail.

Bee is the same. Her name is Beatrice. Call her Bee or get ready to take your medicine.

Like I said, our last names are the same, but the way in which we are related could only happen in the South, in what used to be called the Confederate States of America before the Late Unpleasantness. The Late Unpleasantness is how some of the really old white people in South Carolina still refer to the Civil War. Either that or they call it the War of Northern Aggression. It's obvious to me that they have totally forgotten who started the shooting.

Bee's family would most *definitely* not call it the War of Northern Aggression. If they had a name for it that was different from the Civil War, they might more likely call it the War That Got Us Out of Chains. That's because, way back then, Bee's family members were slaves on my family's plantation. The reason our last names are the same is that slaves didn't have last names, and when they were freed they often took the last names of their ex-owners.

You'd think a history like ours might have kept

Bee and me from being friends, but fortunately a lot of things have changed in the past hundred and fifty years. For example, Reward—the plantation my family owned for three hundred years, ever since my distant ancestors fled from France—now belonged to Bee's family. How all of that came about is related to a mystery Bee and I solved when we first became friends.

Anyway, all that badness between our ancestors has actually made Bee and me close. We were so close, we called ourselves *histers*. It was a word we made up, and it was a combination of *history* and *sisters*. It meant that we were related by things that happened many, many years ago that we had nothing to do with, but which had a lot to do with us and who we were. All that past history bonded us together. Almost like blood kin. Adding to that the fact that we were also best friends, we figure that makes us histers.

Everything I'm about to tell you followed on the heels of the first mystery that Bee and I solved in May of the year we first met. First off, in June Daddy finally opened his eyes and woke up from the coma he'd been in for over nine months. The doctors had told me that waking up from a coma is a lot different than waking from sleep, but I had always dreamed that Daddy would just open his eyes and jump out of bed like he used to when I would wake him up on Saturday or Sunday to go fishing.

That wasn't at all how it happened. It actually took about a week for him to get to where he could talk and sit up in bed, and then it took another week for him to get out of bed. When he finally did get up, he had to hobble around all slow and bent over like a very old man. It made me happy, but it also made me afraid, because I wanted my father back and because the person who had opened his eyes seemed almost like a stranger and not at all like the person in my memories.

But it was Daddy, and after those first two slow weeks, he got to be more like himself almost every single day. He stayed in the hospital most of July in order to do physical therapy and make himself stronger. When he finally came home to Reward Plantation on Leadenwah Island, he and I moved into the old tenant house right next door to Bee in the big house.

If Daddy hated the fact that we had lost the plantation, or that the tenant house wasn't as nice as the big house, which is what everybody called the old plantation house, he never complained. I think he agreed with me that if we had to sell Reward, Bee's family were the perfect new owners.

That July when Daddy was recovering was also

when all the people who had tried to frame Daddy for the theft of Miss Lydia Jenkins's jewelry stood trial. Fortunately, they were all found guilty of grand larceny and also of the attempted murder of Bee, Daddy, and yours truly. The bad guys were all going to be in prison for a good while, which meant Bee, Daddy, Grandma Em, and I could all sleep better at night.

As soon as Daddy came home from the hospital, he and I began taking long walks together every single morning as he worked to build up his strength. I had planted the house garden early in the spring, just like Daddy had always done, so we had lots of fresh vegetables to eat, mostly tomatoes because South Carolina's high summer is too hot for most other things.

On our walks I would blab my head off like I always had with him, but Daddy didn't say as much as he had before his coma. Sometimes he would stop and stare off in space and say nothing at all. At those times, whenever I asked him what he was thinking about, he would shake his head, smile, and say, "Nothing."

Bee's grandmother, Grandma Em, asked us to dinner down at the big house almost every night, and she cooked just about the best food in the whole world. I made sure Daddy ate big meals every day, because he needed to put muscles back on his body. I also made sure he got plenty of sleep, even sneaking his cell phone out of his room at night and putting it back before he woke up the next morning so no one would disturb him.

One day toward the end of August, during the last sleepy days of summer vacation, everything suddenly picked up speed. First off, there was a big robbery that got everybody's attention, when some people stole an armored car full of money. The newspaper had big articles about it because the armored car had supposedly been carrying a lot more money than average—about eight million dollars. The robbers knocked out the guards somehow, and the truck and all its money just flat-out disappeared. Then there was a second robbery just a couple days later, when somebody broke into a gas company and stole one of their trucks. This all went down near our island, which is a place where nothing much unusual ever happens.

And then there was a third robbery, one that got Bee and me way more involved in all the crazy happenings than two twelve-year-old girls ever should be.

The very first sign that all these robberies might affect me came in a way I didn't even recognize when it happened. It was like a line of dark clouds that pop up on the horizon and at first just look like they might bring some rain, but a few hours later, when the wind is snapping trees and the water is rising, it's obvious that those clouds meant something a whole lot worse than a rainstorm. It happened the Saturday morning Daddy came down to breakfast all shaved and showered and wearing a business suit. It was the first time he'd put on his old lawyer clothes, and of course the suit looked about two sizes too big, because he still hadn't gained back his weight. He didn't even bother to put on a tie, because the collar of his shirt was so huge on his skinny neck.

"Where are you going?" I asked, almost too amazed to talk.

"To the office."

"Why?"

He looked at me and gently cleared his throat. "I'm going back to work."

"On a Saturday?" I shook my head. "You can't start on a Saturday." What I really meant to say was that he couldn't start at all, not yet.

Daddy put his hand on my arm and gave it a squeeze. "It's time, sweetheart," he said. "You've taken wonderful care of me ever since I woke up, but it's time I got back into my life."

I felt a big blast of fear, like if he went back to work, something bad was going to happen to him again. I opened my mouth to tell him, but as I did I felt my eyes brimming with tears. I wasn't one of those girls who liked to cry, not a bit, and I pushed back my chair and whipped out of the room and up the stairs. I slammed my bedroom door and lay down on my bed and bawled like an idiot.

A couple minutes later, I heard the door open and then felt the mattress sag as Daddy sat on the edge of the bed. He put his hand on my back and rubbed the way I always like it. "Honeybee, this was always going to happen eventually. I wasn't going to stay home forever. You know?"

I nodded.

"Besides, school starts on Tuesday," he said. "Why don't you and Bee do something today? You two have hardly had time to hang out since I woke up."

"I don't want to," I said, my words muffled by the pillow.

"It's your call, but if I were you, I'd want to take advantage of the end of summer." He gave me a gentle pat on the head. "I'll see you tonight. I'm going to be just fine."

I heard him walk out of the room and go down the

stairs, and a moment later Rufus barked as Daddy's law partner, Custis Pettigrew, drove up to the house. The front door slammed, and then Custis's car door slammed, and then they drove away. I lay there for a long time feeling so afraid, I almost couldn't stand it. I'd had him back for such a short time, and I knew the only way I could make sure nothing bad ever happened to him again was by keeping him right here with me—and now he had gone.

Two

I don't know how long I lay there before the phone started to ring, and I made myself get up and answer it. "Abbey?" a familiar voice said.

I recognized the deep, reedy voice of our neighbor, Judge Gator. Judge wasn't his real first name, and Gator wasn't his real last name. But he was a retired federal judge, and he'd gotten the nickname Gator when he was still the district attorney. Back then the local newspaper had written an article saying Poindexter DeSaussure (that's his real name) was so tough on criminals that a bad guy might just as well put his leg in a big old gator's mouth as to try and get away from him.

He had a voice that always reminded me of pipe smoke and cool evenings and the stories he would tell as we sat together on the joggling board on the front porch of his house. Hearing him on the phone partly snapped me out of my funk.

"Are you in Michigan?" I asked, because it was August and Judge Gator always went up north in early May and didn't come back until October.

"No, I came back early because Yemassee is going to have puppies and I wanted them born here on Leadenwah."

I'm no fool. I was pretty sure Daddy had asked the judge to call me. But I didn't care, because hearing the word *puppies* grabbed my attention. The judge went on to tell me that he'd driven into Charleston that morning for a meeting that looked like it was going to run a lot longer than he'd expected. Since it was a very hot day, he asked if I might be willing to go over to his place and check on Yemassee and make sure she had plenty of water.

I said of course I would, and as soon as I hung up I called Bee. She had never met Judge Gator, as he had already gone up north for the summer by the time she moved to Reward, but she lit up right away when I told her about the puppies. We met at the barn ten minutes later, and we saddled our ponies and headed over to the judge's place.

Judge Gator lived on the neighboring plantation, Belle Vista, which his family had owned for hundreds of years, ever since his ancestors fled France and came to South Carolina. He lived there all by himself ever since his wife had died a couple years earlier. Even though we were neighbors, it still took ten minutes of riding down several dusty trails with the sun beating down on our heads just to get to his fence line, and then another ten minutes once we were through the gate. In case you've never been to South Carolina in late August, we're talking *hot*. Like fry-an-egg-on-a-stone-you-set-out-in-the-sun hot, so by the time we got to Judge Gator's house, Bee and I were both sweating hard, right along with our ponies.

I had known Judge Gator ever since I was a little girl, and I had known his dog, Yemassee, ever since she was a puppy, and now I was excited to think that she was going to have puppies of her own. Daddy used to say that Judge Gator had become a lonely man since his wife died, and I thought it might make him feel better to have a bunch of little animals to care for.

Yemassee was a Boykin spaniel, which happens to be the state dog of South Carolina. Boykins are celebrated for their loyalty; wonderful personalities; beautiful brown, curly coats; and brilliant gold-and-amber eyes. They are even more prized for being amazing bird dogs. Boykins aren't exactly rare, but just like beautiful pianos or fancy cars, they are valued by their owners. And just like any other special thing, the good ones are worth a whole bunch of money.

Yemassee was more than prized; she was adored. Judge Gator liked to say that she was "the best of the best." Sometimes, after Daddy and I had eaten one of his famous fried-chicken dinners, the judge would tell stories of hunting with Yemassee—doves, wild turkeys, and ducks in South Carolina; ruffed grouse in North Carolina and Pennsylvania; pheasants in North Dakota; and chukar partridge in Idaho. In other words, Yemassee was a dog that could pretty much do it all. My father agreed, and he had been bird hunting all his life. He said a dog that could hunt like Yemassee was as rare as hen's teeth, and if you know anything about hens, you know they don't have teeth.

When Bee and I got to the house, we tied our ponies by the back door, where the judge kept a big water trough in the shade of a huge live oak. We let the horses drink and went into the kitchen to find Yemassee, but strangely she didn't bark or come to see who was there.

"Yemassee," I called.

"You think she could be having her puppies already?" Bee asked, when she still didn't come.

A shot of excitement ran up my back as we started to search from room to room. The judge's house was old, and there were lots of creaky floorboards. Everywhere we looked we saw shelves full of books and more books stacked on tables. The air smelled like a combination of musky old stuff, damp dog, pipe tobacco, and gun oil.

"Check the closets and under the beds," Bee said. "Maybe she made a nest."

We looked everywhere, but no dog. Finally we had only one more room to check, the big sunroom at the far end of the house. When I looked in there, I noticed one of the sliding glass doors standing open a few inches, and I had my answer.

"Where do you think she is?" Bee asked.

"She's gone hunting," I said.

Bee screwed up her face and looked at me. "Huh?"

Sometimes I forget that Bee moved here just a couple months ago from the Atlanta suburbs. She doesn't know much about dogs or hunting.

"Dogs never understand when they get left home for their own good. Sure as anything, she watched Judge

Gator get dressed to go into town this morning, and the moment he drove away, she ran around the house until she found a door that wasn't shut tight enough."

"How do you know?"

I laughed. "Because she's done it before, and Boykins have heads like rocks."

"Meaning they're stubborn?" Bee asked.

"Yeah."

"Takes one to know one, I guess."

"Aren't you the comedian."

"Truth hurts, girl."

I looked at Bee and tried to think up some smart comment, but then I gave up and laughed. She was totally right. The fact was, Yemassee would do whatever Judge Gator asked, but if anybody but Judge Gator called her and expected her to come, they'd best have a big piece of steak in their hand. That's just the kind of dog she was, and I guessed Bee was saying that was the kind of girl I was, too. I would do pretty much anything to make Daddy or Bee or Grandma Em happy, but other people—like my teachers—would say I was as hardheaded as a piece of wood and usually did exactly as I pleased. Maybe it did take one to know one.

Bee and I walked out the sliding glass door and looked toward the shadiest parts of the yard, but we didn't see a dog. I called Yemassee's name several times.

"You think she went far?" Bee asked.

I shrugged. "Hard to say. Girl dogs don't usually wander, but Yemassee's different. The judge says she brings home souvenirs from all over Leadenwah."

"What kind of souvenirs?"

"Bones, mainly, but one time she brought home a bridle. Another time some people must have been skinny-dipping in the creek because she brought home somebody's boxer shorts."

Bee laughed. "I'd like to have seen that."

"We need a treat," I said, walking back inside and getting some bacon from the fridge.

Outside again I shouted Yemassee's name and this time called out, "Treat!" just to make sure she knew there would be a reward. After another minute we went back through the house and out onto the front porch. I called out, "Treat," in that direction, and a minute later Bee pointed down the drive. "Look."

I saw something in the distance coming slowly up the allée of live oaks. For a second I wasn't certain it was even a dog, but as the shape drew closer I could make out Yemassee's dusty brown fur.

She was over a hundred yards off, and it looked like she was half dragging, half carrying something that was long and awkward, because she would stop every fifteen or twenty yards, drop it, then pick it up again.

"Looks like she dug up a dinosaur bone," Bee joked.

"Must be quite a prize," I said with a laugh. Yemassee looked so dusty and tired that I guessed she must have taken a long jaunt to get that thing.

Then another motion caught my eye. A vehicle was coming up the driveway at a fast enough clip to throw a big rooster tail of dust. At first I thought it might be Judge Gator rushing back from Charleston, but when it got closer I knew it wasn't, because Judge Gator had an old Mercedes station wagon, and this was a white pickup. The driver had to be an idiot, because even from where we stood on the porch I could hear the wheels slamming hard in the ruts.

"That truck's going to hit Yemassee!" Bee cried.

I stared, realizing she was right. The Boykin spaniel was in the middle of the drive, and the truck was coming up on her real fast. It appeared that the driver didn't see her. I opened my mouth to scream, but at the last second the driver slammed on his brakes and slid to a stop just behind Yemassee.

Two men jumped out of the truck. I couldn't see them well because of all the road dust they had kicked up, but the driver looked sort of short and thick. The passenger was taller and a good bit skinnier.

"Here, doggy," one of the men called, but not the way a person calls a dog. It was more of a *I'm going to beat you when I get my hands on you* voice.

Something about the man's tone sent a shiver down my back, and I grabbed Bee's shoulder and made her squat down with me behind a couple big pots of geraniums.

Yemassee totally ignored the man, and both of them started to chase her. Right away I realized that they had to be after the thing she was carrying. I would have laughed at the sight if the men hadn't looked so angry.

As we watched, the fat man stayed behind Yemassee, while the skinnier man veered off to one side and ran sort of parallel to her. He seemed to be trying to head her off so she couldn't reach the house.

Yemassee wasn't fooled. She changed direction, managing to hold the thing in her mouth as she trotted off between several of the live oaks that lined the drive. I was about to call out and tell the men to stop chasing her, tell them I could get her to drop the thing by offering her a treat. I opened my mouth, but then I saw the rifle in the taller man's hands, and the words froze in my throat. All I could do was watch in horror. A voice in my head kept telling me that this *could not* be happening, but it was.

Yemassee was about to duck under the pasture fence when the man raised the rifle to his shoulder.

That broke my paralysis. "No!" Bee and I shouted at the same instant. We stood up and leaped off the porch, running toward Yemassee. The fat man glanced in our direction then said something to his partner. I never heard any sound from the gun, but in the next instant I saw Yemassee sit, then collapse onto her side and lie still.

I was already in tears, crazy with anger. I was going to run up to the man with the rifle and kick him in the crotch as hard as I could and then keep on kicking until he cried like a baby. My tears were coming so fast, I couldn't see. It was like driving in a car through a rainstorm with the window wipers off.

Bee was running beside me. I could hear her crying and yelling something, but I paid no attention. I didn't know she was telling me to stop until she tackled me and we both fell in the dirt.

"What are you doing?" I shouted. "Get off!"

But she wasn't getting off. She was keeping me pinned with all her strength. "Stay down!" she kept saying.

I got an arm free and was about to pull a good

handful of her hair when I paused for half a second and looked at her face. She was a teary, snotty mess, but she kept telling me to stay down like it was the most important thing in the world. It finally got through to me.

"We can't help Yemassee if we get shot too."

I raised my head and blinked through the dust at the two men. The one with the gun sidestepped over, dropped the gun to his hip but kept it aimed at us, and picked up whatever Yemassee had been carrying.

Then the fat man did something that surprised me. He walked over and picked up Yemassee, then backed toward the truck.

"What are you doing, man?" the tall man said, loud enough for us to hear.

"This is a Boykin spaniel!" the fat man said.

The first man grumbled as he hurried back to the truck, but the other man put Yemassee gently on the floor of the cab, then climbed in over her and slammed the door. The driver spun the wheel hard, spinning his tires and kicking up another huge cloud of dust, and the truck skidded and fishtailed in a turn and roared back out toward the county road. There was so much dirt in the air that Bee and I couldn't see a thing.

When I finally managed to get out from under Bee,

I jumped up and started to run back toward where we had tied the ponies.

"What are you doing?" Bee demanded as she ran behind me.

"I'm going home to get Daddy's bullwhip," I panted.

"Your dad doesn't have a bullwhip," Bee said.

I stopped and spun on her. I *hated* the way she is totally rational at times when I wanted to go totally crazy. "Well, we have to do *something*!"

"Did you even see which way the truck turned when it got out to the road?" she asked.

"No," I said.

"Well, if we don't have any idea who they were or which direction they turned, there's no way we're going to catch them, is there?"

I threw my hands in the air. "So what are we going to do?"

"Go back home and tell Grandma Em."

"And what's she going to do?"

"Call the police."

I scowled. Even though I saw the sense in what Bee was suggesting, I liked my idea of crotch kicking and bullwhipping a whole lot better. Still, we did what she suggested, meaning that we jumped on the ponies and raced back toward Bee's house.

Bee's dad owned a lot of companies, but his newest one was in India. He was over there a lot of the time, making sure everything was set up right, and Bee's grandmother took care of her at home. Grandma Em was a big deal in both our lives, because neither Bee nor I had a mother. Bee's mom and brother died in a terrible car accident just about a year earlier, and my own mother died of cancer when I was very young. Grandma Em was always there for us, and she always knew what to do when something would go wrong.

We barreled back along the dirt path and up the plantation drive, and the ponies were slick with sweat as we skidded them to a stop in back of the big house. We tied the ponies by the fountain, where they could get a drink, and we went boiling up the back porch steps and into the kitchen. Grandma Em was at the stove making meatballs in tomato sauce for dinner.

"Whoa, there," she said as we threw open the door and let it slam behind us. "Take off those dirty boots before you go another step."

"Forget the dirt!" Bee cried. "We were over at Judge Gator's and we saw two men in a truck drive up and shoot Yemassee!"

Grandma Em was tall and imposing. My father said she had a regal bearing, meaning that something about her reminded him of a queen. She was very kind and loving most of the time, but when Grandma Em got angry, her voice was as hard and scary as a marine drill sergeant's. Also, when people didn't do what Grandma Em wanted, her eyes got a steely glint that could make an alligator turn tail and run away. I think Grandma Em got that way from being an elementary school principal for all those years when she lived in Atlanta.

Right then her eyes went ice-cold. "They *shot* his dog?" she asked in disbelief. "Are you girls making this up?"

"No! We have to call the police!" Bee insisted. Her face was slick with a combination of smeared tears and sweat from the afternoon heat and our hot, dusty gallop back from Judge Gator's. "Tell them to come right out."

Grandma Em never panicked or got rattled. Even then with Bee racing off at the mouth about a pickup truck and a gun and Yemassee getting shot, she just held up a hand to quiet us down.

"*Exactly* what did you see?" she asked.

"We *told* you what we saw!" Bee's eyes were starting to spill tears again. "Yemassee got shot!"

"Okay, okay," Grandma Em said in a soothing voice. "Is that what you're going to tell the police?"

"Yes!" I exclaimed.

"Now, girls," Grandma Em said, "didn't you two start a business sometime early in the summer?"

I threw up my hands. What did that have to do with anything? "Yes, ma'am, but—"

"And what was the name of that business?"

"Come on, Grandma!" Bee cried. "Just call!" She rolled her eyes in frustration.

"Answer the question, please."

"Force and Force Investigations," I said. It was the business Bee and I had started in June, after we solved the Mystery of Felony Bay. It had seemed like a fun idea at the time, but as the summer wore on and Bee got a pony and we rode together every day and swam in the river off the plantation dock, we hadn't thought about investigating a single thing, other than spying on some baby ducks that lived on one of the plantation ponds.

Grandma Em went on. "So, if an investigator calls the police to report a crime, what kind of information would the police expect them to provide?"

Bee and I shrugged.

Grandma Em threw up her hands in frustration. "What were they driving?"

"A pickup truck."

"What color?"

"White."

"What make?"

Bee and I looked at each other then shook our heads.

"Any lettering on the side?"

"It kicked up too much dust to see," Bee said.

"Was there anything else unusual about the truck that you can recall?" Grandma Em prodded. "Light bars on top? Rust? Dents?"

I closed my eyes and tried to picture the truck, and after a second I nodded. "It was one of those trucks that have double back tires on each side."

"That's good," Grandma Em said. "There aren't as many of those as there are regular pickup trucks. What about the men in the truck? Had you seen them before?"

I shook my head.

"Were they Caucasian, Hispanic, African American . . . ?"

"White," Bee said.

"How old?"

Bee and I looked at each other. "One was maybe forty or fifty," I said.

"He had dark hair and a big belly," Bee said. "I could see that much."

I nodded, remembering how the man's navy-blue

T-shirt bulged out over his belt like he had a watermelon in there.

"What color hair?"

"Black," Bee said.

I closed my eyes. "But shiny bald on top," I added.

As we were answering her questions, Grandma Em had grabbed a pad of paper and was jotting everything down. "What about the second man?" she asked.

"He was younger," I said. "Maybe in his twenties or thirties."

"Tall and thin with lousy posture," Bee added.

"He was the one who shot Yemassee," I said.

"Hair?" Grandma Em asked.

"I think it was blond," I said. "But it was hard to tell for sure, because he wore a baseball cap." I closed my eyes and recalled a pair of wraparound sunglasses on a narrow face. I fixed both of the men in my mind, and I imagined having a bullwhip in my hands when I ran into them again.

Three

Cyrus Middleton was our new Leadenwah Island deputy, since the old deputy, Bubba Simmons, was in prison. Cyrus was very tall, with shoulders that reminded me of big fence posts. He had a dark face, as round as a full moon, and not a bit mean like Bubba's had been. He had huge hands, and he moved slow and talked even slower, so it would have been easy for someone who didn't know him very well to think Cyrus wasn't very smart. That would have been a big mistake. Cyrus might have moved slowly, but he didn't miss anything that went on around him.

Cyrus was on the front porch of the big house

interviewing Bee and me and taking notes when Daddy and Judge Gator drove up the plantation drive. Daddy must have called him after I told him what happened. Judge Gator jumped out of his old Mercedes station wagon and strode up onto the porch, looking like someone I'd never met before. With his gray hair, bright blue eyes, his easy way of talking, and his deep, gravelly laugh, Judge Gator is one of the kindest people I've ever known. Today his mouth was a hard line, and his blue eyes were flashing so bright, they reminded me of sunlight glinting off the blade of a freshly sharpened knife. Today he looked as mean as his nickname.

Daddy came limping behind the judge, moving a lot slower, still using a cane to walk and looking as if his day at the office had tired him out. Bee and I stood up, and Cyrus also stood.

"They shot my dog?" was the first thing out of the judge's mouth.

"Yessir," I told him. "I'm sorry."

"Not as sorry as they're gonna be," he growled. He glanced at Cyrus. "Excuse me, deputy. I apologize if you have already covered all of this, but I need the girls to tell me everything."

Grandma Em had written down all the details she'd made us recall, and Bee had typed them up on the computer and printed them out. We handed our report to Judge Gator, and he read it over fast, then pointed his finger at one line in the report and raised his eyes to us.

"You said their gun made some kind of funny noise. What kind of noise?"

When Grandma Em made us think hard about all the details, Bee and I remembered that we had never heard a gunshot. "I didn't hear anything," I said. "But Bee said she thought it sounded like somebody spitting."

The judge frowned. "Was Yemassee knocked backward by the shot?"

Bee shook her head. "No, sir. She just sat down and then keeled over."

The judge rolled his jaw around, and his eyes got very small. "Sounds like it was some sort of tranquilizer gun," he said quietly. He looked at Daddy and at Cyrus. "I bet they wanted my puppies."

Cyrus nodded. "Last year we had about five Boykins stolen right here on the island. I wonder if it could be those same people stealing dogs again."

The judge nodded. "I think that's got to be it. And I'm betting it's somebody local."

A few minutes later, having promised to put out a notice to all the local police departments to be on the lookout for a heavy-duty white pickup with the two men we had seen, Cyrus left. Grandma Em invited Judge Gator, Daddy, and me to stay for dinner and share the spaghetti and meatballs she had made earlier. We accepted in a blink, even Judge Gator, because nobody, and I mean nobody, turns down a chance to eat Grandma Em's cooking. Not even somebody whose heart is breaking because his best friend has been stolen.

While the grown-ups sat on the front porch and had cocktails before dinner, Bee and I walked out onto the dock and watched the tide go out and the fiddler crabs scooting across the pluff mud. For a time neither of us said a word. I kept thinking about what it was like for me when I almost lost Daddy, and I knew Bee was probably thinking the same thing, maybe what it was like when she lost her mom.

"The judge's wife died a couple years ago," I finally said. "Now Yemassee is all he's got."

Bee nodded. "I was thinking the same thing. I mean, losing a relative is terrible, but if you lose the only living thing that helps fill an empty house, is it any less bad because it's a dog?"

"Know what I think?" I said.

"What?"

"Grandma Em said there aren't nearly as many

six-wheeled pickups around as standard ones. And Judge Gator said he was sure someone on this island stole Yemassee. There are only so many places where someone could park a truck like that . . ."

Bee scowled and nodded and threw a stick in the water and watched it float out of sight. "Force and Force," she said, after a long silence.

I looked at her, and suddenly I got it. My eyes widened, and I snapped my fingers. "Yes!" I said. "Force and Force Investigations. We'll find Yemassee."

Nobody said much at dinner because, in spite of how good the food was, we all felt the judge's sadness. Afterward the judge drove Daddy and me home to our tenant house, and when we got out of the car we stood outside and watched the judge's old Mercedes disappear down the drive.

"I feel terrible for him," Daddy said.

"Me too," I said, but I kept the news to myself that Bee and I were going to find Yemassee and get her back. If I'm being honest, I had a feeling Daddy wouldn't want me poking around in strange backyards, and I didn't want him to squash our investigation before it even got off the ground.

When the judge's car finally disappeared, I looked

up. It was one of those clear nights when the stars lay bright in the sky and seemed closer than they really were.

"I'll let Rufus out, and then we can spot constellations," I said as I ran up on the back porch.

Rufus is our black Lab, and he was standing right at the door, whapping his tail against the wall and the refrigerator. When I opened the door, he bounded out, racing around and watering the trees, the tires of Daddy's Suburban, and all the corners of the house. Just in case anyone forgot exactly which dog owned the property.

"In a few minutes," Daddy said. "I have some work I have to do."

"It's Saturday night," I said. "Today was only your first day back at work."

He nodded. "And I'm already busy, honeybee."

I didn't want to hear that. Before Daddy's coma we used to play a game to see which one of us could identify the most constellations. Daddy always used to win, but I had been getting better.

Before he could go inside, I lay on my back in the grass and looked up at the sky. "There's Aquarius," I said, pointing at some stars that ancient sky watchers thought looked like a man pouring water on the ground. To me Aquarius looked more like a sad dog with a big head. Rufus came over to me for a scratch, and I pointed his head up at the sky.

"There's a sad dog," I told him. "Maybe it's Yemassee." Rufus apparently did not care about sad dogs. He gave his head a quick shake and nosed me for more scratching. "There's Cepheus," I said, pointing up again at a constellation named for some old king but that looked to me like a kindergartner's drawing of a house.

"They're the only ones I can see," Daddy said, but I could tell he wasn't thinking about constellations.

I sat up and looked at him.

"Sorry," he said. "But I've got a bail hearing and motion I've got to prepare for."

"Bail?" I said. I didn't know much about law, but I knew bail was money that got posted to get people out of jail after they got drunk or in a fight. "Who's in jail?"

Daddy gave me one of those looks that said I should know better than to ask. "A client."

He turned and went up the steps and into the house, and I sat there feeling scared. I tried to tell myself it was stupid to feel like that, probably selfish too, because I could tell he was excited to get back to work, but sometimes feelings and facts are just different.

When I walked in the house a few minutes later, Daddy was already hard at work, sitting at the kitchen table, his glasses perched on the end of his nose as he read from a law book and made notes on a yellow pad. He had turned on the TV and tuned to the local evening news.

"Hey," I said. "I guess I'll go to sleep." Bee and I had a big day planned for tomorrow, because we were going to start looking for Yemassee.

"Okay," Daddy said, sort of half paying attention, but then the news lady on TV said something about the "recent Leadenwah County crime wave." She said there had been no progress in finding the stolen armored car, but the police expected breaks very soon because, "You just can't make an armored car disappear." The news lady switched to the robbery at the Old South Bottled Gas Company, and suddenly Daddy's head jerked up and he grabbed the remote control and hit the record button.

According to the announcer, police believed the thieves had been looking for money, and when they didn't find any, they had stolen a truck loaded with tanks of gas. She said a man named Willie Smalls had been arrested in connection with the robbery.

I knew a man named Willie Smalls who lived in a

little tumbledown cabin not too far from Reward. The Willie Smalls I knew was slow talking and very slow thinking, but he was nice and honest. I was sure he couldn't be the person they were talking about on TV. That was until I looked at Daddy again.

"Is Willie who you're bailing out of jail?" I asked.

Daddy glanced at me, hesitated, and then nodded.

My jaw dropped. "Willie wouldn't steal anything."

"I happen to agree, but Willie was the night watchman, and the robbers used his keys to get into the building, so it doesn't look good."

My brain was suddenly moving in a different direction. What kind of risks was Daddy taking getting involved in something like this? What kind of bad things could happen? "I didn't think you did that kind of law, you know, where people get arrested."

"Criminal law," he said. "I usually don't, but Willie's dirt-poor. If I didn't take his case, I didn't know if anyone would." He must have seen the worry on my face, because a second later he said, "Don't worry, kiddo, I'm not taking any risks with a bail hearing. I'm just trying to make sure Willie gets a fair shake."

He turned his attention back to the TV, where the announcer was saying the thieves hadn't been very smart, because all the tanks had Old South Bottled Gas written on the sides, and the truck had the same thing written on the doors. She said the police expected to find it pretty soon.

A second later the television showed a clip from a security camera of two men wearing clown masks as they came through a door and walked toward a parked truck. The clip also showed a third man slumped on the ground with his back against a wall and what looked like a bottle of liquor in his hand. Even though the camera was up high on a wall, I recognized Willie Smalls. He appeared to be sleeping.

But that wasn't the amazing thing. That came when one of the men took off his mask in order to get into the truck they were going to steal. The picture was grainy, but even so there was no mistaking who it was.

"That's him!" I shouted, pointing at the tall, skinny man on the television. "That's the guy who shot Yemassee!"

Four

The next day was Sunday, and Bee and I got up early, packed snacks and water, smeared on sunscreen, and met at the barn a few minutes after seven. We brought along a map of Leadenwah Island, and our plan was to ride down every single back road and try to spot the white truck.

As we saddled the ponies Bee said, "You really think that truck is on the island?"

I nodded. "I bet it's near wherever Yemassee found that white thing she was carrying," I said. "Probably the men who stole her saw her as she was digging it up. If we just ride around long enough, I bet we'll spot them."

Leadenwah Island is about seven miles long and three miles wide, and it forks like a pair of rabbit ears about halfway out, creating two separate points of land that jut out into the river. The point nearest to Reward is called Bishop's Point. The farther point is called Sinner's Point.

Like a lot of places in our part of the country, Leadenwah Island had a fair number of people who lived in small houses or double-wides set close to the road. We figured that if the fancy pickup with the double back tires belonged to one of them, it would be easy to spot. But there were also a fair number of folks with plenty of money who lived on much bigger places, and while the two guys we saw hadn't looked rich, it definitely wasn't out of the question.

Even before we got to the end of the plantation drive and onto the township dirt road, I could sense Bee already starting to worry. When I glanced over at her, she was chewing her lip. "What?" I asked.

"Most of these big places are set pretty far back from the road," she said.

I shrugged. "So?"

"Gonna be hard to see a truck if it's parked all the way in the back."

"Yup," I agreed.

"So we're gonna trespass?"

"Can you think of any other way for us to spot that truck?"

Bee thought about that for a long moment. "I guess not," she said at last.

We rode out the plantation drive, then turned left on the township dirt road. We went past several of the neighboring properties without even turning our heads, because we knew the people who lived there and the people who worked for them.

When we hit the paved road that ran down the center of the island, we turned left. A big tractor trailer overflowing with a load of freshly dug dirt passed us heading toward the mainland, and we had to close our eyes and turn our heads away from the blowing dust. That was the only vehicle we saw until we came to the Y intersection and went left, heading toward Bishop's Point. After that we saw an SUV or two and some pickups. None were white, and besides that I recognized the drivers and waved. A tractor with a big cutting bar passed us on its way to mow someone's fields, and we waved at that driver, too.

Once we were on the point, we stayed on the main road and then turned down the first of the narrow dirt roads that went toward the water and started to search for the white truck. We checked the small places close to the road and skipped past the first couple big places because, again, we knew the owners and the people who worked there. The third large property was one we didn't know anything about.

Old families still owned a lot of the larger properties on Leadenwah, but increasingly, as people would pass away, strangers from Atlanta or Charlotte or New York would buy them. Some of the newcomers spent a lot of time here and really became part of island life, but there were some, like the owner of this plantation, who didn't seem to care much about getting to know us locals.

"Ready to do some exploring?" I asked.

"Okay, but if somebody comes out and starts screaming at us, you're doing the talking," Bee said.

Bee might have been the worst liar who had ever been born. I'd figured out pretty soon after we'd become friends that whenever we had to fib our way out of a tough spot, I was the one who had to do it. "No problem," I said.

The property where we stopped had a couple fancy gateposts marking the entrance. A pair of wrought-iron metal gates would have been closed if the owners were away, but today they were open. We turned our ponies into the drive and started down the long allée of live oaks. The branches formed a high canopy over our heads, and Spanish moss hung from them and waved in the breeze.

We rode in silence for a ways, but then Bee asked, "So what are you going to say if the owner threatens to call the police?"

"Easy," I said. "We're going to say that we thought one of our classmates lived here."

"And what if we run into those two men?"

I shot her a sideways glance but didn't say anything because I'd been worrying about the exact same thing. We were getting farther and farther away from the township road, and I was growing more and more nervous.

Plantation is a Southern word that basically means "big farm." In my opinion plantations are the most beautiful places in the world, lush and green with fields of crops, and pastures full of animals, and ponds that twinkle in the sun, and pretty houses, and lots of flowering trees. A plantation is the opposite of a suburb. There aren't any nearby houses or neighbors you can run to for help, and once you get far enough away from the road, people driving past in cars wouldn't be able to see you at all.

Therefore, if you went riding up the driveway of a plantation where someone wanted to hurt you, it could be real dangerous. It hadn't even been four months since some bad people had tried to kill Bee and me on our own plantation, so I knew I wasn't being a weenie.

"Um, there's one thing I kind of forgot to tell you," I said.

Bee looked at me and wrinkled up her face like she knew it was going to be bad. "What?"

"I saw one of those men on TV last night. They didn't just steal Yemassee. They also robbed that gas company."

Bee's eyes went wide. "Those guys saw us!" she exclaimed. "And now you tell me they're also like major criminals? Are you seriously crazy?"

"This isn't just about Yemassee," I told her. "It's about a man named Willie Smalls and Daddy." And I told her about who Willie was and about Daddy's bail hearing. "If we can find the men who did all this, it'll help Daddy out, and he can get back to doing the kinds of things he was doing before, not getting all mixed up in this dangerous criminal stuff."

She looked at me, and her eyes narrowed. She huffed some air out her nose and shook her head. "I must be crazy to be your friend," she said.

Up ahead of us the line of live oaks seemed to

stretch forever. Cows and horses grazed in the pastures on either side. We had ridden a good quarter mile off the county road before some barns came into view on our left. They were pole barns, the kind with just a roof and no walls, so I could see through to the other side. I looked hard for any sign of a white pickup truck but saw nothing other than tractors, mowers, and assorted farm equipment.

"Is this far enough?" Bee asked, her voice tight with anxiety.

That was when I heard the bark. A second later four or five big dogs came around the corner of an outbuilding and headed straight for us. Judging by their angry sounds, I didn't think they were coming out to say hello.

"I think this is plenty far," I said as I wheeled Timmy around. I didn't even have to kick him, because it was clear he didn't want any more to do with those dogs than me. Even Bee's pony, Buck, was fast on his feet for once as we started to gallop down the drive toward the township road.

Ponies are fast, but their legs aren't as long as horses' legs by a long shot. For a few seconds it seemed like the dogs were going to catch us because we had to start from a dead stop and they were already running. I felt a twinge of something close to panic as I heard the barks getting closer, and I kicked Timmy hard. The barks stayed close for several more seconds, then finally they began to fade. When I felt like I could risk it, I looked back and saw that the dogs had stopped and were standing with their tongues lolling out as they watched us leave.

Once we were back out on the township road, Bee and I reined in our ponies and let them catch their breath. "That wasn't overly successful," I admitted.

Bee gave me a cool look. "I'd say your brilliant plan of trespassing onto people's property and then claiming to be lost is almost guaranteed to get us bitten or shot."

I bit back my normal response. Bee could definitely be a bit of a wuss, but in this case I couldn't argue. Anyplace we trespassed was going to have dogs, or worse, a hothead with a rifle or shotgun. I should have known that in the first place. After all, we *were* in South Carolina.

"Okay, change of tactics," I said. "From now on we'll circle the fence lines and try to find a way in through the pastures. We'll stay out of sight better and be farther away from the buildings and the dogs, but we still ought to be able to spot the truck."

Bee mulled over my suggestion for a few seconds then gave an uneasy shrug. "We'll try it," she said. "But we stay away from swamps."

Bee harbored an unholy fear of snakes and any other critters that like to hang out in swamps. Also a few months earlier we'd almost been eaten by a huge alligator named Green Alice.

"Deal," I said, happy that she was still willing to come along.

We continued down the dirt road. For the next five hours, every time we came to a large property, we skirted the fence lines until we found an unlocked pasture gate. It took longer that way, but we stayed out of sight and managed not to get chased by any more dogs or any crazy owners. We spotted plenty of trucks but not a single new white pickup truck with a set of double back tires.

The day continued to get hotter as we searched. The sky was cloudless, the breeze nonexistent. We found several places to water the horses, but by late afternoon we were tired, frustrated, sunburned, mosquito-bit, out of snacks, and very sweaty.

As we plodded along the dusty road toward home, I got out the map and planned our next day's exploration. Little did I know what lay ahead. If I'd had any idea, I think I might have given up any hope of rescuing Yemassee and maybe even of trying to help Daddy.

Five

The next morning Bee met me at the barn at seven, just like we had planned, but she told me she couldn't go riding right away. Grandma Em had a new project she was working on, and she wanted Bee to learn about it. I was invited, too, she said.

"How long will it take?" I asked.

"We're leaving in just a few minutes, and Grandma Em promised it would take only about two hours. She wants to get done before it gets too hot."

"I guess I'll come," I said. I didn't want to give up two hours of looking for the white truck, but I sure didn't want to go snooping all alone, either.

We went out into the pasture, got our ponies and put them in their stalls so we wouldn't have to waste time catching them later on, and just about the time we finished, Grandma Em drove up to the barn in a car I'd never seen before. A stranger got out of the driver's seat and introduced himself. "I'm Professor Emmitt Washburn, girls," he said.

The professor was a tall, thin African American man with his hair all black and gray, which made me guess he was probably about as old as Grandma Em. But I also noticed that his eyes had the kind of glint in them that you'd expect to see in an excited kid and not in an old person. It made me like him right off. He opened the door for us, and Bee and I climbed in the backseat.

As we started driving, Grandma Em swung around in her seat and told us that Professor Washburn taught at the College of Charleston, and the two of them were working on a project to identify all the old slave graveyards on Leadenwah Island, mapping them out and making sure they were protected. The professor started talking, too, and he told us how slave graveyards were the places where slaves used to bury their dead. Unlike white people's graveyards, which had big fences around them and lots of fancy headstones, the slaves had nothing to mark their graves except things they planted and bits of pottery and other small items that over the years rotted away or got broken or covered with leaves. Because of that a lot of the slave graveyards had become lost and forgotten, and sometimes farmers or builders would find them totally by accident.

Grandma Em jumped in and told us how most people would try to respect the graves and would call the proper authorities so the bodies could be dug up if necessary and reburied someplace else, but how other people didn't. Hearing the two of them and how excited they sounded, a person might have thought a slave graveyard was the most interesting thing since sliced bread. I glanced over at Bee a couple times, and she shrugged at me as if to say, *Who knew what was going to get two old people excited?*

I looked out the window the entire time we drove, because we were heading in the same general direction Bee and I had ridden the day before and I was hoping to catch sight of the white pickup. We went a little farther out on Bishop's Point, turned down a dirt road, and drove until we came to a small turnoff. There wasn't anything that looked like a graveyard, but then I spotted a narrow path leading off the road into a square of land that looked a little different from everything else around it.

The professor parked, and he and Grandma Em got some colored tape from the trunk. Bee and I followed them down the path to where some bushes and trees had recently been cut, and the ground changed. Inside the cleared area were a number of spots where the earth had sunk down a few inches. The sunken areas were all the same rough shape, maybe a couple feet wide and five or six feet long, and most of them had a yucca plant growing at one end. It took only a second or two to realize I was looking at graves.

Professor Washburn and Grandma Em went around the edges of the plot, looking at the ground with great care and tying the colored tape to different bushes and trees to mark off a rough square. When they finished, Professor Washburn came to where Bee and I were standing, and he led us to some of the depressions in the ground, where he squatted down and felt around under the thick litter of fallen magnolia leaves, finding several small pieces of pottery.

"Very often either yuccas or cedars or magnolias were used to mark the graves because the slaves had no gravestones, and these plates and cups would have been some of the very few possessions the slaves had," he said. "Their loved ones put them around the graves to help the spirits on their journey."

I looked at the small pieces of plates or cups the professor had found, but when I looked over at Bee, she was staring at a piece of a broken bowl and I could tell her mind was going a million miles an hour.

Grandma Em came up and put her hand on Bee's shoulder. "You okay, sweetheart?" she said gently.

Bee nodded but kept staring at the little shard. "This could have belonged to somebody in our family," she said, after a few moments.

"Yes," Grandma Em whispered.

A few seconds later, when we put all the pieces back under the leaves where the professor had found them, I felt bad, like I wanted to apologize for something. I wasn't quite sure how to put it into words, so I said nothing.

When we finished at the grave site, Grandma Em and Professor Washburn dropped us off at the barn. Bee had been quiet on the way back to the plantation, and she was still quiet when we walked back into the cool darkness of the barn. At one point as I saddled Timmy I felt Bee's eyes on me, and when I turned around she was staring at me the way she might have looked at a complete stranger.

"What?" I asked, even though I was pretty sure I

knew what the problem was.

Bee took a deep breath and let it hiss out. "I'm just trying to understand how anyone could have treated people so badly."

I nodded and felt my shoulders sag. I knew she was talking about my family and her family. It was the same question that had been digging away at my brain ever since we'd found those pieces of pottery. That was just about all those people had owned, a plate and maybe a bowl, along with the shoes on their feet and the shirts on their backs. "I don't know," I said at last. "But I'm sorry."

Bee came over and gave me a soft punch on the shoulder. "I know," she said. "It's just that, living here, all that stuff seems so close sometimes."

"Yeah," I said.

Wanting to find a way to break the awkwardness, I took out the map from a day earlier, where I had marked off the roads we'd already gone down. "Look, we've done these," I said, showing Bee. "Okay with you if we start here?" I pointed at the dirt road where we'd been just a little while earlier. I hadn't seen any place on that road before we reached the slave graveyard that we needed to explore.

Bee shrugged. "Sure," she said.

We led the ponies out of the barn and mounted up, and just as it always did, the act of getting up on Timmy's back made me feel better. I looked overhead and saw that the sky was cloudless, which meant it was going to be another scorcher. Even the breeze seemed so tired out by a long summer of hot days that it could hardly be bothered to blow.

My brain sort of went to sleep in heat, and I forgot about everything but riding ponies and finding Yemassee as we trotted off the plantation, to the end of the dirt road and then along the paved county road, once again seeing very few other cars or trucks. A horse van went by, a pickup and a tractor, and then another of the big tractor trailers roared past loaded with dirt that blew off the top and burned our eyes and noses. Just like yesterday we saw no white pickup trucks with double rear tires.

We took the fork to Bishop's Point and turned onto the road I had marked, and when we passed the slave graveyard, we once again began riding the fence line of the big properties. We stayed at it for nearly three hours and covered four more roads before we stopped to eat the snacks we had brought along and give the ponies a rest.

"Sure would be nice to take a swim this afternoon,"

Bee said as we mounted again.

"Yeah," I said, wiping the sweat from my face with the tail of my T-shirt. "But we should keep going a little while longer," I said. "School starts tomorrow, and we won't have very much time to search."

Bee sighed and slumped in her saddle. "We haven't seen anything except some big houses and barns and a bunch of tractors and other farm junk and about twenty snakes."

I felt just as hot and tired as she did, but I kept thinking about the judge and about Daddy, who I was pretty sure had gotten a ride into his office with Custis and was working all day getting ready for tomorrow's hearing. "None of the snakes were poisonous," I said.

"But they all scare me. I hate them, even the ones that aren't poisonous, even their little tiny babies."

"But don't you feel sorry for the judge and Yemassee? Don't you want to help Daddy and Willie Smalls?"

"Yeeessss," Bee drawled out in her most frustrated tone. "You know I do."

"Then we need to keep looking."

Bee let out a sigh, but she gave Buck a kick and headed down the road beside me.

We rode for another couple hours until we had covered nearly everything that was left of Bishop's Point.

I felt as hot and cranky as Bee and just as frustrated, because we hadn't seen a thing that resembled the big white pickup truck or a stolen dog. We were getting close to the end of the very last road on the point when we came to another large property.

"This has to be the last place," Bee said. "If I don't get in the river soon, I'm gonna die."

"Okay," I promised.

The property had a white fence along its front and an electric gate across its drive. Low, swampy land ran along the near side of the property, and that meant snakes and alligators, so we stayed on the road and went all the way to the far corner. When we reached it, we saw that the fence turned ninety degrees and ran through fairly dry ground as it headed toward the back of the property and the Leadenwah River. A few yards beyond the fence line what looked like a rutted dirt path also ran back through the palmettos and wild oleander, seeming to run roughly parallel to the plantation's fence.

I turned and waved to Bee, who had stopped about twenty yards behind me. "This is the last place, and we have an easy way to sneak along the side."

Bee was slumped in her saddle in a way that let me know she was more than ready to quit. I started into the dirt track, but when I glanced back again she still wasn't following. "Look," I said, pointing, "solid ground. No swamps in sight. Last place, I promise. Come on."

Bee pressed her lips together, swallowing whatever complaint she wanted to make. After a second she gave Buck a reluctant kick and caught up. We started up the path but went only a few yards before the vegetation thickened, pressing close on both sides and cutting off our view ahead or behind. It also killed the breeze, and the air became steamy and close, smelling of mud and rot. Mosquitoes buzzed around my exposed skin, and behind me I could hear Bee slapping as they landed on her.

When I glanced down at the ground, it looked like a set of big tires had recently gouged the soft dirt. It made me a little nervous, and I tried to look through the thick undergrowth for signs of a shanty or a rusted trailer up ahead. It sure didn't look like we were riding into a place where someone actually lived, but it wasn't unheard of to have your basic hillbilly or redneck living next door to a fancy plantation.

The plantation fence was somewhere off to our right, but the trees were too thick to see it. To my dismay the dirt track bent to the left, heading away from where I sensed the fence had to be, and at the same time it also seemed to get darker and spookier.

"Abbey!" Bee whispered behind me. "I think we ought to turn around."

I was afraid, too, but Bee was making me act braver than I felt. "Just a little farther," I insisted.

"Forget it!" Bee's pony came to a stop behind me.

My sense of unease had blossomed like a magnolia flower in full sun, but I thought about Daddy and Willie Smalls and Yemassee and Judge Gator and tried to fight off my fear.

I turned in my saddle and whispered, "Maybe this is where the truck is. How are we ever going to know if we don't keep going? Remember all the people we need to help."

"We won't help anybody much if some crazy old man lives back here and he shoots us."

I looked at her, wishing she wouldn't talk like that, because it just made it harder for me to keep my own fear under control. "Just a little farther."

Bee scowled, but when I nudged Timmy forward with my heels, she came, too. The ground under us was getting wetter, because I could hear the muck sucking at our ponies' hooves each time they took a step. When I glanced down, I could see that whatever had recently driven in here had also sunk deeper and deeper into the mud as it continued onward.

Up ahead the path turned even sharper to the left, completely cutting off our view. It felt like flies were buzzing in my stomach, but I said nothing, afraid if I did Bee would turn around and trot back to the road.

As we came around the curve, my heart went straight into my mouth, and I jerked Timmy to a halt. Up ahead, so deeply buried in the undergrowth that it was almost invisible, I saw the rear end of what looked like a white pickup truck. My heart went even further into my mouth when my gaze dropped and I saw the set of double rear tires.

I turned in the saddle and looked back at Bee, who hadn't seen the truck because I was blocking her view. What she didn't miss was that my eyes were as big as saucers. "What?" she demanded.

"It's the truck!" I mouthed.

Bee's jaw dropped. She wheeled Buck around, and for a half second I was afraid she was going to start galloping in the other direction.

"Wait!" I hissed.

We fast walked the ponies back around the curve until we were out of sight of the truck, and the whole time my brain was racing. I had no idea where the driver and passenger might be. Maybe they'd been close enough to overhear us. I held my breath, listening for voices or the truck engine starting up, but the buzzing of mosquitoes was all that disturbed the heavy silence. After a few seconds my stomach began to unclench.

"I don't think they're here," I whispered. "The truck is just, like, jammed really far into the bushes. It looks like they drove it as far as they could and left it."

Bee let Buck take a couple steps back toward the road. "Fine. We need to call the police! Let them figure it out!"

I had to admit what she was saying made sense. That was what Daddy and Grandma Em would want us to do. But I started to wonder about Yemassee. "What if Yemassee is here right now? What if she's right around the corner tied to a tree? What if they just left her there and she's thirsty and doesn't have any water? You want to leave when we could maybe get her and take her home right now?"

"Abbey, sometimes you're impossible. Those men could be sitting there with guns, just waiting for someone to come looking for them."

I shook my head. "If they were here, we would've heard them because they would have heard us."

I climbed down off Timmy, tied his reins to a bush,

and tiptoed back toward the curve. "Abbey!" Bee whispered, but I ignored her. I told myself to relax and think about what was obvious: the truck engine wasn't running, and it was way too hot for people to be sitting in a truck cab getting eaten alive by mosquitoes.

I came back around the curve feeling like I had a whole covey of quail fluttering around in my stomach, and I peeked at the truck from behind some bushes. Something about where it was, the way it had been left, something I couldn't put my finger on, wasn't right. I could see lots of bugs buzzing around the open window. They were either bees or flies, and I wondered what had gotten them all stirred up.

When I glanced back, I was surprised to see that Bee had climbed down off Buck and followed me. She gave me an angry glance but then crept forward and peeked at the truck with a frightened expression. "What's it doing there?" she whispered.

I said nothing as I started toward the rear of the pickup, not wanting to go but dragged forward by a growing sense of dread. The mud was deeper here, and my feet made loud sucking noises as I lifted them, but the closer I got, the surer I was that nobody was there.

I could see the bugs more clearly. They were flies— black and heavy and moving with a blowsy slowness as if they had eaten big meals and were too stuffed to fly fast.

I took another couple of steps, and a terrible smell hit me. It hit Bee, too, because she made a choking sound. We probably would have smelled the stink earlier but for the total absence of a breeze in the heavy undergrowth. I took another step, and the smell grew worse.

"Breathe through your mouth," I whispered to Bee.

"What is it?" she whispered.

It was a stomach-twisting stench that reminded me of a dead deer I had found in the woods one time, and it was definitely coming from the truck. "I don't know," I whispered, but I had a terrible, heart-wrenching certainty that Yemassee had died, that the men had panicked for some weird reason and abandoned their truck here with her body inside.

I felt tears bunching at the corners of my eyes, but I sucked a huge breath through my mouth and moved toward the back of the truck, intending to take a quick look and confirm my fears. When I put my head over the side, to my great relief I saw that the truck bed was empty. There was nothing in it but a couple of two-by-fours and some empty burlap sacks.

My relief caused me to forget the stink, and I took a

fresh breath through my nose that nearly made me gag. I had to bend over and take a few quick gulps of air through my mouth to keep from barfing.

"You okay?" Bee whispered.

I nodded, but then I noticed that the driver's side window was open. For a second fresh panic welled up inside. Maybe the driver was sitting there waiting for us after all? No way, I thought. There was *absolutely* no way anybody could sit quietly and breathe in this stink.

I took another couple steps forward, and that was when I saw the hand. I choked back the scream that tried to break from my throat.

"What?" Bee whispered.

I shook my head for silence, because somebody was in the truck after all. They must have seen us sneaking up the whole time, but if they had, what were they waiting for? I told myself to turn and run, but my feet were half stuck in the mud, and I was nearly paralyzed with fear.

My eyes stayed riveted on the hand. A fly landed on it, then another. Strangely the man didn't twitch his fingers to get them off. His skin color was also strange. It was too white, so pale it reminded me of a lemon ice pop.

This close the smell was even worse. Even though I

breathed through my mouth, the stink was so powerful, I could actually taste it. When my fear finally eased
enough for me to move, I took another step closer.

I never took my eyes off the hand, not for a single
second. I was only a couple feet away now. There were
raw places where the flies had been eating the skin. I
knew it had to hurt like crazy, but the hand still didn't
move.

I glanced around, saw a small dead branch, and
picked it up. Trembling, I gave the hand a little poke
and immediately jumped back, nearly falling as the
mud sucked at my feet. The hand still didn't move.

"What are you doing?" Bee whispered.

I had no voice. My words had seized in my throat.
I stepped back toward the door and poked the hand
again, harder. Nothing. I turned around, no longer caring if I made noise, because I knew it didn't matter.

"What?" Bee demanded.

I tried to explain, but before I could I bent over and
threw up.

Six

An hour later Daddy, Grandma Em, and Judge
Gator were all gathered around Bee and me. We
were back out on the county road, where our
ponies had been tied up in some afternoon shade and
where someone had brought a big bucket of water for
them to drink. Police cars were parked all up and down
the road with their flashers going. Our local deputy,
Cyrus Middleton, was there along with state police
officers and some men from an organization called
SLED, which stands for State Law Enforcement Divi-
sion.

An ambulance had arrived a few minutes earlier,

and it was backed up to the dirt path with its rear doors standing open. The two attendants had carried a stretcher back through the mud to fetch the body, but they hadn't returned yet. All we knew so far was that the man in the pickup truck was dead, but we didn't know who he was. I'd never gotten close enough to get a look at his face, so I didn't know whether he was one of the two men who had stolen Yemassee and robbed the gas company.

Daddy and Grandma Em were fit to be tied by everything that had happened. Grandma Em hovered near us with her arms crossed, glaring at every policeman who came within twenty feet, as if she held each one of them personally responsible for leaving a dead body in the woods where we could find it. But she saved all of her worst glares for Bee and me. Daddy was probably as upset as Grandma Em, but he kept it inside better. Even so, I knew I was in serious trouble.

Judge Gator was nearly as upset as Grandma Em. He had been pacing up and down ever since he had arrived, stopping every couple of minutes to shoot a look at Bee and me, give his head a shake, then start pacing again. "If I'd had the slightest inkling that you two girls were going to go out searching for a couple dognappers who also committed grand larceny," he said, "I would have locked you in your bedrooms myself."

Before either of us could say for the fortieth or fiftieth time that we were sorry, one of the SLED officers came over to where we were standing and motioned for Daddy, Grandma Em, and Judge Gator to speak with him privately.

Grandma Em shot us one more look. "You two girls stay *right* here," she snapped, then marched over to hear what the policeman had to say. The policeman talked for a moment, and then they went back and forth with a lot of whispering. At one point Grandma Em started to hiss at the policeman in a way that reminded me of an angry cottonmouth.

Finally Daddy turned and gave me a worried look. I had already guessed what they were all talking about. I could feel a whole bunch of butterflies swarming in my stomach, but I walked over to where they were all talking. As I got close they all stopped whispering and turned.

"They want one of us to look at his face, don't they?" I said to Daddy.

"You are *not* doing it!" Grandma Em snapped.

"That's right, honey," Daddy said. "You don't have to do it."

I looked at the policeman and nodded. "I'll do it," I

said, my voice coming out choked. Part of me was terrified and totally grossed out at the idea of looking at a dead man's face. The other part of me needed to know if this was one of the men who had shot Yemassee.

Daddy held my hand and walked with me, and we went to stand at the back of the ambulance. About twenty yards away, I could see the two ambulance attendants struggling as they carried the stretcher, since they couldn't roll it on the muddy ground. Their feet were caked with brown goo, but the sheet covering the body remained perfectly white.

They came up to us and put down the stretcher very gently. The policeman put his hand on the corner of the sheet and paused. "Are you ready?"

I nodded and swallowed hard as my stomach bucked and churned. I had seen plenty of dead animals on the side of the road and deer hanging after hunters had shot them and plenty of dead doves and quail, but I had never seen a real dead person before.

When the policeman peeled back the sheet, I gasped. The man's face was whitish yellow. Thankfully his eyes were closed. I could see a small hole in the side of his forehead just in front of his ear. There was blood on his shirt, but not much. He had blond hair and a narrow face.

"Do you recognize him?" the policeman asked in a gentle voice.

I sucked down more air, once again tasting rather than smelling the man's terrible stink. I didn't open my mouth until I trusted myself to speak without barfing. "Did he have sunglasses on?" I asked.

The policeman re-covered the face with the sheet, then he turned and walked over to another policeman. They spoke for a second, and the policeman returned holding a plastic bag in one hand.

"He was wearing these," he said, holding out the bag and showing me a pair of wraparound sunglasses.

"Can you show me the face again, please?"

He pulled back the sheet a second time and held the bag with the sunglasses in front of the face.

I nodded. "That's the man who shot the judge's dog."

"Are you sure?" the policeman asked.

"Yessir, absolutely."

When we finally finished and were able to start home, we loaded the ponies into the horse trailer Daddy had brought over. It was the first time he had driven since he'd woken up, but I didn't say anything, because I was already in enough trouble as it was. Daddy and I drove back in the Suburban while Bee and Grandma Em followed in Grandma Em's car.

"You okay?" Daddy asked as soon as we got under way.

I nodded.

"It must have scared your pants off to find that body."

I nodded again. "Pretty much."

"You know, speaking of being scared, I know you're worried about me going back to work."

I glanced over at him but didn't say anything.

"Being scared cuts both ways. To think that you and Bee have been riding around this island trying to find a dog that was stolen by some dangerous criminals—" He slapped the steering wheel and shook his head. "I've got to be able to trust that you have more sense than that."

"Sorry," I said, my voice little more than a whisper. I hated the way he could say things that made me look at situations from a different angle and see what I'd missed.

"As you know, Willie Smalls has been accused of helping those men, but I believe he's innocent," Daddy went on. "I'm trying to keep Willie from going to jail. Willie isn't any risk to me, but those other men are a *big* risk to anybody who finds them."

"Yessir."

"So no more looking for Yemassee." He glanced over at me, and his eyes were hard. "Understood?"

"Yessir."

When we got back to Reward, Daddy stopped at the barn so I could unload the ponies. Bee showed up a couple minutes later, and we washed Timmy and Buck, then fed and watered them and finally oiled our tack.

"Did Grandma Em give you a really hard time?" I asked as we worked.

Bee nodded. "She didn't yell as much as make me feel terrible for scaring her so bad."

I nodded. "Me too. Are you grounded?"

"No, but I can't go look for Yemassee anymore. What about you?"

"Same."

When I walked into the house a few minutes later, Daddy was just ladling some steaming okra gumbo that Grandma Em had given us into two bowls, and we sat together at the kitchen table. Grandma Em's cooking helped make me feel better, just the way it always did. In addition to the gumbo, Daddy had tossed a quick green salad and pulled a baguette out of the freezer and stuck it in the oven to warm up.

I hadn't really noticed, but he was doing more and more every day. He had his trial tomorrow, and I knew without even asking that he would be going to the office day in and day out from now on. I didn't like it, but I realized there was nothing I could do to keep it from happening.

As we started to eat, Daddy cleared his throat in a way that told me he had something more to say. "I know you've got school starting," he began. "But when you're not doing homework or sports, I want you to stick close to Reward. It looks like we have a killer running around on this island, and until the police catch him, I don't want you roaming."

Now that I had sat down and started to eat, I realized how exhausted I was. Finding that dead body had taken every bit of fight out of me. Rather than arguing, I just nodded. "Yessir."

I finished my dinner and was about to excuse myself and head up to bed when I realized Daddy had grown very still and intense.

"Something the matter?" I asked.

He looked up, blinking his eyes like he'd been someplace far away. "I was thinking about the gas-company robbery and stealing the truck, and Willie

Smalls, and then those men taking Yemassee. I'm try-ing to see some connection between all those things." He shook his head. "None of it makes sense, but I'm thinking maybe they're connected."

"How do you mean?" I asked. In spite of how tired my brain was, I had been wondering the exact same thing.

"I can understand somebody getting Willie drunk so they could steal his keys and then breaking into the gas company. They probably hoped to find a bunch of cash lying around, and when they didn't find any, they stole one of the trucks."

"But why would they steal Yemassee?"

"Exactly." He took a spoonful of gumbo but then stopped with the spoon just an inch or two from his mouth. "I didn't pay much attention at the time, but didn't you say Yemassee was carrying something in her mouth?"

I nodded. "Something long and white."

Daddy finally put the spoon in his mouth. When he swallowed, he asked. "Maybe something that came off a gas truck?"

He looked at me, and I looked back at him. My eyes were growing so heavy, I could barely see. Neither one of us had any answers.

When I climbed under the covers that night, I let Rufus get on my bed. I almost never did that, because Rufus had a tendency to cut farts that would choke a horse. Still, in spite of the risk of getting gassed, I needed his warm, furry body to cuddle.

I closed my eyes and had to concentrate hard to keep the image of that dead man's face from rising up. Rufus's clean dog smell and the steady sound of his breathing helped drive it away.

The other thing that helped was planning what I would do later on that week. Daddy had forbidden any more searching for Yemassee. He was only trying to protect me, and he was going to be really mad and really disappointed if he found out I had disobeyed. But I also knew he was taking a lot of risks himself by getting involved with Willie's case, and when an adult is too stubborn to admit they need help, sometimes kids have no other choice but to disobey. Thursday was going to be the first day I wouldn't have after-school stuff, and I decided that afternoon, with or without Bee, I would take a riding tour. I tried to ease my conscience by telling myself I wouldn't be *totally* disobeying. After all, Daddy hadn't told me not to ride, just to stay close to Reward.

Leadenwah Island was a small place, and so

anywhere I went on the island would be "close" to Reward in most people's minds. Bee and I had checked out Bishop's Point, but we hadn't looked on Sinner's Point, and I knew that was one of the places Judge Gator liked to walk Yemassee. It made sense that if she had gone hunting that day, she might have gone back to some place she'd been before, where she liked to sniff around. It had been a long time since I had ridden over to Sinner's Point and explored all the back roads. It was time to do it again.

Of course I would only be enjoying the beautiful scenery. If I just *happened* to spot a stolen Boykin spaniel, well *that* would be a complete coincidence. If I just *happened* to rescue the stolen Boykin spaniel, it would only be because, under the circumstances, it was the absolute right thing to do. Ditto if I just *happened* to spot the shorter man who had been in the truck that took Yemassee and told the police where to find him. After all, Daddy needed help, even if he wouldn't admit it, and Judge Gator needed his dog back. In my mind both of those things were important enough to risk disobeying a direct order from Daddy.

Seven

In the morning **Daddy did** something else that shocked me: he drove Bee and me to school on his way to work. I sat in the front seat and watched him like a hawk, making sure he was okay. I felt bad about thinking it, but I almost wished he couldn't drive because it would mean he couldn't go to work very easily.

In the afternoon I had tennis practice, and Bee had volleyball, and then Grandma Em brought us home. Miss Walker's is a serious school, and since they believed in starting the year off with a bang, we both had a ton of homework. Daddy worked late, because in addition to Willie Smalls's hearing, he called me to say that he already had another big case. I was afraid that was going to happen a lot. People thought Daddy was a great lawyer, and probably a lot of them had been waiting for him to get back to work.

I ate dinner at Bee's house that night and also on Wednesday. Bee and I had a few classes together, like history and math, but I took Spanish and she took French, and then we played different sports, so we saw each other only for a few quick minutes between classes. Even at dinner we didn't have much chance to talk, because Grandma Em filled up the first meal telling us about her slave-graveyard project, and then on Wednesday Professor Washburn showed up for dinner.

He brought a little bouquet of flowers for Grandma Em, and from the way he smiled and jumped up from the table and pulled out a chair every time Grandma Em wanted to sit down, I almost got the impression he wanted to be her boyfriend. The whole thing struck me as funny, because I never imagined old people having boyfriends or girlfriends, but then I started to watch the way Grandma Em acted with Professor Washburn. She was all smiles and twinkly eyes as soon as we sat down. It was kind of embarrassing to watch two old people acting that way. I could sense Bee having the same reaction. I didn't dare look in her direction, because I knew if we made eye contact we would start giggling and never stop.

In spite of how weirdly funny I thought Grandma Em and the professor were, I found their conversation pretty boring as they talked about this graveyard and that graveyard and which ones had been mapped out and which ones were still rumored to exist but remained undiscovered. Blah, blah, blah.

I was tired and thinking about all the homework waiting for me back at my house. By the time we finished the main course, it was everything I could do not to let out a big, rude yawn.

I glanced at Bee, but unfortunately she was sitting with her hands folded in front of her, looking across the table at the professor just like she was some straight-A student, which of course she was. She even asked a couple of questions, and I wanted to kick her under the table, because she was making dinner last even longer.

I looked away from her, back at Grandma Em. I was desperate to catch her eye and let her know that I needed my dessert so I could get to studying. The professor was still in the middle of droning on about different parts of the island. He'd been talking about Bishop's Point earlier and was now talking about Sinner's Point. I was barely listening, but then I caught the words "Hangman's Bluff."

In spite of myself, I said, "Pardon?"

Professor Washburn smiled, seeming delighted that I was suddenly showing interest in graveyards, but I wasn't. It was just that his mentioning Hangman's Bluff made me remember something totally different.

"Daddy won a big lawsuit over that property a couple years earlier," I said.

"It's a large, undeveloped property," the professor said.

"A man named Mr. LaBelle used to own it," I said.

"Yes," the professor said. "I believe he still does. Are you suggesting that's a place we should explore?"

I shuddered and shook my head, not because of Yemassee or Hangman's Bluff or the dead body we had found, but at the memory of Mr. LaBelle's daughter, Donna, who had gone to Miss Walker's, where Bee and I went, and had been the nastiest girl I ever knew.

"Mr. LaBelle isn't exactly friendly with our family," I told him. "Daddy sued him back when Mr. LaBelle wanted to build a whole lot of condominiums out on Hangman's Bluff."

"I think I remember reading about that," the professor said.

"Mr. LaBelle was trying to get around the laws against building stuff."

"Zoning laws?" asked Grandma Em.

"Yes, ma'am," I said. "Mr. LaBelle had a lot of money, and Daddy says he must have thought the people on Leadenwah were a bunch of ignorant hicks and were too stupid to stop him from doing whatever he wanted. The zoning laws say Leadenwah is only allowed to have farms and plantations and homesteads, not shopping centers and condominiums. A bunch of people on the island hired Daddy to be their lawyer, and he beat Mr. LaBelle like an old drum. Mr. LaBelle ended up losing a whole lot of money, and they sold their house and moved away."

Just about then Grandma Em glanced at her watch. "Oh my, the time has totally gotten away from me. You girls have homework. Why don't you take your plates in the kitchen and get your dessert there? Then Abbey can leave whenever she needs to."

I didn't need any more encouragement. I thanked Grandma Em for dinner and said good night to the professor, then followed Bee into the kitchen.

"At least we don't have to talk about graveyards anymore," I whispered as we got ice cream out of the freezer and Bee cut slices of freshly baked pecan pie.

"Did you really think that stuff was interesting?"

"I thought you did, too, when the professor started talking about Hangman's Bluff."

"Not because of graveyards," I told her. "Only because it reminded me of Donna LaBelle."

"I don't know her."

"Obviously, because she moved away before you came, but just hope she never moves back."

I shuddered again, and I suddenly got one of those weird feelings that seem to come out of nowhere. It told me that where Donna was concerned, luck was running against me. That was even more reason for us to take a little pony ride out to Sinner's Point, just to make sure there was no sign that the LaBelles had come back to Leadenwah.

When I whispered that to Bee, she looked at me like I was out of my mind, and in hindsight maybe she was right.

Daddy was in the kitchen eating a salad and watching the Weather Channel when I walked into the house. The announcer was talking about a storm that seemed to be heading someplace between central Florida and North Carolina.

I had been mulling over the bad feeling I had in my

bones as I walked home. "Is there a way to tell if some-body is getting ready to build something new around here?" I asked.

He glanced away from the TV. "Hello to you, as well. Thank you for asking if I had a nice day. Yes, I did. And I hope you did."

I went over and gave him a kiss on the cheek and said a proper hello. "Now can you answer my question, please?"

He kept one eye on the TV as he talked. "Building permits have to be filed with the county. They're public information."

"Could you look and see if anybody has got build-ing permits?"

He gave me a squirrelly look. "Why would I be doing this?"

"At dinner tonight Grandma Em and her friend were talking about slave graveyards."

Daddy nodded. "She's told me about her project. It sounds interesting. Desecrating old graveyards has been a problem around here for a long time, but it's against the law. If people are building a new house or devel-oping property and they find a graveyard, they have to report it, and then they have to properly rebury the bodies. Is that what you're trying to find out about?"

"No," I said.

Daddy turned away from the TV by then and gave me one of his looks. "What's going on in that head of yours?"

"The professor brought up Hangman's Bluff and said he thought Mr. LaBelle still owns it. I thought he'd sold it."

Daddy shrugged. "I'm not really sure what's happened to that land. What do you care?"

"You know how people get hunches?" I asked. "Well, I got a hunch that maybe Donna LaBelle hasn't gone away for good."

Daddy rolled his eyes. "Donna LaBelle, your old nemesis." He laughed. "I'll look into what's happened to that land, but it's going to be a day or two." He pointed at the TV. "It might take even longer if this storm throws a wrench into everything and we have to spend time closing shutters and tying things down outside."

"Could Custis check on it?"

Daddy shook his head. "He's helping me with this new case, and he's still at the office even as we speak. I'll get to it in a couple days. I promise."

I nodded and said good night and went up to finish my homework. Afterward I got Rufus on the bed and tried to dream about Yemassee, but instead I had a nightmare about Donna LaBelle.

The next day was Thursday, the first afternoon of the week when neither Bee nor I had after-school sports, which meant there was free time for riding. Grandma Em picked us up after school and brought us out to Leadenwah. We had no chance to make plans in the car because we weren't supposed to go looking for Yemassee anymore, and also because Grandma Em had the radio turned up pretty high, listening to reports about a tropical storm.

The announcer said the storm had stalled off the coast, and its direction had become very difficult to predict. Even so, conditions were excellent for it to strengthen into a hurricane. He warned that people all along the East Coast should make sure they had plenty of batteries and fresh drinking water in their homes and to keep their car tanks filled with gas.

I wasn't very concerned from hearing all this stuff, because it seemed like every year in the late summer or fall we had at least one close call from a hurricane or tropical storm. When I looked overhead, all I could see was typical South Carolina blue sky, which made it even harder to get very worried. The day was sunny and perfect, and I was excited to go riding.

As soon as I got to the house, I let Rufus out to pee, then changed out of my uniform and into riding clothes, loaded a day pack with water and snacks, and headed to the barn. I saddled Timmy, and then because Bee hadn't shown up yet, I also saddled Buck. I was finished with both horses by the time Bee walked into the barn.

At first she didn't say anything, just walked over to where I had rested my day pack on top of one of the tack trunks. She lifted the flap and saw that I had put water and snacks in there for both of us.

She turned and gave me a look. "Grandma Em just gave me a whole fresh lecture. She says we're not to go looking for Yemassee."

I gave an innocent shrug. "I just thought we'd explore a different part of the island. No problem with riding the roads, is there?"

She put her hands on her hips. "One dead body wasn't enough?"

"We're not going near where we found that guy." As I said it an involuntary shiver ran down my back. "That would be way too creepy. I thought we should ride over to Sinner's Point."

"We?"

I shrugged and smiled. "I got you snacks and water."

One of Bee's eyebrows shot up. "You want to go looking for Yemassee," she said.

Knowing Bee's instinct was usually to do exactly what she'd been told, I said, "We're not going to go snooping around looking for anything. I just want to, you know, go down some of the roads we never go down."

"Just ride? No trespassing? No creepy dirt tracks? How far from Reward?"

"Not far." I held up my hand and put two fingers in the air. "Scout's honor."

Bee finally gave in, and we mounted and rode across the island toward the farther of the two rabbit ears that form the island's points. Each fork is fairly narrow, with just a single paved road running down the center and dirt roads cutting across and heading toward the water.

The main paved road had little traffic, just a couple pickups and SUVs that had drivers I knew. It was typical Leadenwah, except for another one of those huge tractor trailers full of dirt that went past. Just like the other day, the truck was going fast with loose dirt blowing from the top.

It got into our eyes and our mouths and made us cough, and it struck me suddenly that all this dirt had to be coming from a place where somebody was doing a lot of digging. And who would be digging except somebody who was building something? And weren't they building something pretty big to haul this much dirt? And wasn't there just one person I knew of who'd tried once before to build something big on Leadenwah? Mr. LaBelle had gotten stopped the first time, but what if he was trying to sneak some kind of building project in and get it done before Daddy and other people could stop him? If that was the case, it meant Donna LaBelle might be back on Leadenwah. My stomach clenched at the thought.

My mind had started to race, and I was wondering when Daddy would have time to try and find out who was doing all the digging, when Bee said something that stopped my thoughts dead, almost like somebody shoving a stick into the spokes of a bike. "What did you just say?" I asked.

"I just asked if your family doesn't have some old journals and other stuff about the plantation. I was thinking I'd like to look at them."

I turned and looked at her. "Why?"

"Remember that paper we got assigned today in history?"

Earlier that day we'd been given an assignment to

write a biography about someone in our family. We had to research it, either through interviews with the person if they were living or through journals, letters, or other sources if they were dead. Most of our classmates were going to write about their parents or grandparents, because it was easier to do someone who was alive, but Bee's mother and brother had been killed in a car accident just a year earlier. Doing a biography on either of them would mean digging up a lot of painful memories, and I knew she wasn't ready. Maybe even researching her father or Grandma Em would be coming too close.

"Daddy gave them to the Historical Society."

"Do you think they'd let us look at them? I was thinking about all those graveyards Grandma Em and the professor have been protecting, and about my ancestors who are buried there. I'd like to learn anything I can, like where they came from in Africa, what year they came here."

My stomach clenched at the thought of going through those old records, because they talked about when members of my family bought members of Bee's family like they were cattle.

"Okay," I said, trying to sound a lot more comfortable about it than I felt. "I'll help you. Maybe I'll find an ancestor of my own to write about from the same time period."

I glanced at Bee, who had the kind of look on her face that people get when they're about to go into the doctor's examination room and they know that what's about to happen is necessary but also that it's going to hurt. It was exactly the way I felt, because I was pretty sure it was going to hurt both of us.

We rode for nearly two more hours that afternoon, trotting the dirt roads, skirting the large plantations, but I kept my word, so we no longer snuck back along the property lines. It wasn't nearly as exciting as the poking around we had done the previous times, but there were no dead bodies, either.

Riding on the roads, we saw nothing but distant houses and fields and barns, intermixed with woods and an occasional swamp. The sun was starting to drop low in the sky, with deep pools of shadow gathering under the live oaks. We were going through the motions of looking for Yemassee, but I knew in my heart that we probably weren't going to spot her. Even so, riding a pony beats doing homework any day of the week.

We had covered almost all the roads on Sinner's Point, and it was getting toward time for dinner. Bee was yawning in her saddle, and I expected her to suggest we turn around and head for home, but she surprised me.

"That horrible girl you talked about last night?"

"What about her?"

"Was she *really* that awful? You don't usually let people get under your skin that bad."

"Just close your eyes and imagine a wicked witch with blond hair, pink bows, and flouncy dresses. Also, she's got a pretty little smile that hides her snake fangs."

Bee laughed. "Did she live around here?"

"You mean at Hangman's Bluff?" I shook my head. "Nobody lives there. It's out at the end of Sinner's Point on the only road we haven't explored yet."

Bee shrugged. "We've come this far. Let's check it out."

I nodded eagerly, and we turned and trotted the ponies to the last dirt road on the point. It was narrow and shaded by the overhanging branches of ancient live oaks. Turning into it, we went past a few double-wides set close to the road and several small houses, then a long space of empty woods with no houses at all. Finally we came to the end of the road, where a length of shiny chain lay in the dirt between two old gateposts. A sign said trespassers would be prosecuted. A padlock hung from one of the gateposts, and a bunch of heavy tire tracks had churned up the dirt, as if big trucks had been driving in and out of the property recently.

"That's Hangman's Bluff?" Bee asked.

I nodded.

"How did it get that name?"

"They used to hang people here."

"What kind of people?"

"Like runaway slaves and criminals," I said, my voice low.

Bee looked at me for a long moment, and I knew she was wondering about her own family.

"Then it used to be a tomato farm, until Mr. LaBelle bought it," I continued.

Bee pointed to a rotting wooden sign on a nearby tree. The paint was nearly worn away, LaBelle Vista just barely visible. "This is where he wanted to build the condos?" she asked.

I nodded.

"He sounds like a real jerk."

"Yes, but not half as bad as his daughter."

Knowing my tendency to exaggerate, Bee cocked her head. "You're talking about a *kid*, not Adolf Hitler."

"Pardon me," I said. "Donna was nice . . . if you like two-faced, stuck-up blond-haired jerks dressed in pink and green who go around school telling people that your father is a monster who's trying to destroy her whole family."

Bee laughed, but then her expression grew serious,

and she nodded toward the tire marks. "All those trucks full of dirt, you think they could be from here?"

I shrugged. "Daddy always said he wouldn't trust Mr. LaBelle any farther than he could throw him. Maybe we ought to ride in a little ways and see."

"We promised your dad and Grandma Em we wouldn't trespass anymore."

"But that was on plantations. This isn't a plantation, right? It's not the same thing."

"What about the No Trespassing sign?"

"That's probably been here a long time," I said, even though I thought it looked pretty new.

I was talking braver than I felt, and as I took a long look down the dirt track that disappeared into the thick trees of Hangman's Bluff I felt an involuntary shiver, and this time it had nothing to do with Donna LaBelle. There was something about the place that gave me the willies. The drive that led into the property was narrow and deeply shaded. Even the trees seemed spooky. Hung with lots of Spanish moss, their massive old limbs drooped low, as if the evil things that had happened out there centuries ago had dragged them nearly to the ground.

It was getting to be dusk, that time of early evening when everything, even the breeze, becomes dead still for a few moments. With night coming this particular spot at the end of this nearly deserted road suddenly felt even creepier. Still, we had come all this way. It seemed a shame just to turn and leave.

"I bet, even if people were here, they've gone home," I said, trying to talk my way through my jitters.

"Then why isn't the chain locked?" Bee asked.

"Just in case I'm wrong, we'll tie the ponies here and go in on foot."

We were about to dismount when we heard an engine, and a second later a pickup truck appeared, coming toward us along the dirt track. Bee raised her eyebrows and gave me a look. "Everybody's gone home, huh?"

The truck came to a stop a few feet short of the chain. My heart went into my mouth as the driver got out. For a second I was afraid it might be the fat man who had stolen Yemassee, but he was someone I had never seen. He was tall and heavyset, with swelling shoulders and a lump for a belly, the kind of man who looks like he has a lot of fat over a lot of muscle. He had thick lips and a gnarled old peanut shell of a nose, and heavy black stubble covered his cheeks. He walked toward the chain with his head down and, guessing he was about to lock it back in place, I kicked

Timmy and rode toward him.

"Excuse me, sir," I called out.

The man raised his head and gave me an unfriendly look. His hair hung in a greasy mullet beneath an Atlanta Braves cap. More tufts of black hair poked out all around his collar, and when he opened his mouth, his teeth were crooked and yellow.

"Whatta you want?" he demanded.

"I wondered if we could ride our ponies out to see the water."

"They teach you to read where y'all go to school?"

"Yessir."

He pulled the chain out of the dirt and pointed at the No Trespassing sign. "What's it say?"

I shrugged. "I just wondered."

He turned back toward the pickup truck and gave a whistle. A second later a big Doberman pinscher shot out the open driver's side door and came trotting toward us. Maybe it was my imagination, but its eyes seemed locked on me. My stomach started to flutter. Both Timmy and Buck tried to wheel, because the dog seemed to be picking up speed as it came. Part of me wanted to let Timmy run, but the other part of me was frozen in disbelief. We were on the county road. This man wouldn't dare let this dog attack us. I hoped.

The dog didn't make a sound, which made it all the more fearsome. The man waited until the Doberman had almost reached us. "Halt!" he commanded. The dog stopped on a dime, but then it raised its lips to show its fangs, a dog message that said it would like nothing better than to rip out my throat.

"You still wonder, girlie?" the man asked.

My heart was thumping hard. I was angry as a stepped-on cottonmouth, but there was nothing I could do. "I guess not," I said in a tight voice.

"Good. Now git 'fore Leaper here gets too excited to hold hisself back."

Bee and I turned and started for home, neither of us saying much. Bee was smart enough not to give me a lecture about how dumb I'd been to want to sneak into Hangman's Bluff. For my part I was still boiling mad, but I also knew how lucky we had been to see the man and the dog before we were on the property. I sure didn't like the idea of having Leaper try to tear off my leg.

We were only about halfway to the county road when we spotted a car. It was facing toward us, and even though the daylight was getting dim beneath the heavy overhang of live oaks, its lights were off. Since it hadn't been there when we rode in, it must have come in after us.

The car was sitting on a slant, and one of its front tires was flat. The driver's door was open, and a woman was standing beside the car. She wore a dress and high heels, and she was talking into her cell phone, waving her free arm as if she was very angry. She was having a hard time walking in her heels in the uneven dirt, and I saw her stumble a couple times.

The woman stopped talking after a few more seconds and listened, but whatever the person said on the other end of the phone only made her madder. "You get here right now!" she said, her voice getting loud enough for us to hear. "I don't *care* what you're doing! Nothing is more important than getting this tire fixed!" She paused, looked at the phone, then yelled into it, "Don't you *dare* hang up on me! Hello? Hello?"

She glared at the phone for a few seconds, then started jabbing the buttons with angry pokes. When someone answered, I knew it must have been the same person she had just been speaking to, because she started right in shouting, "Get here *now*! Do you hear me?" She punched a button, then took her phone and threw it down in the dirt. She tried to give it a kick, but she missed and almost lost her balance.

Bee and I looked at each other, uncertain. The woman hadn't yet glanced in our direction, but she would any second. Normally we would have tried to help without even thinking about it, because that's what people do in the country. But this woman seemed so crazy-angry that it might be smarter to sneak around her.

We sat there another moment. Finally Bee said, "We can't just leave her here, can we?" She didn't sound any more eager than I felt.

"I guess not," I muttered.

We nudged our ponies forward. As we got closer I could see that the car was a Mercedes. When we were still about twenty-five yards away, the woman turned her head so I could get a good look at her profile. I felt a shot of cold dread, and as I reined Timmy to a stop I knew all my evil premonitions had been spot-on. "Oh, no!" I whispered.

Bee looked at me in surprise. "Wh—" she started to say, but I shushed her and started to turn Timmy around.

"Quick! Let's get out of here," I whispered.

"Why?" Bee asked.

It was already too late, because the woman had turned toward us. For a split second she appeared relieved, but then her eyes focused on my face, and her lips curled into a sneer of recognition.

"*You*," Mrs. LaBelle spat, like it was my fault her tire had gone flat. "What are *you* doing here?"

In the South certain people liked to say that "breeding trumps all." I'd never liked that expression because I thought it was snobby. It sounded to me like people were being compared to dogs or horses, and a lot of fine dogs and horses probably should have been insulted. According to that "breeding" baloney, the way a person, especially a kid, was supposed to show "the quality of their bloodline" was through their manners. Therefore, a "well-bred" kid would always be polite to an adult, even if they thought the adult was a stupid, rude idiot.

People who believed that stuff would never have mistaken me for "well-bred," because I had always been lousy at faking what I felt. And I wasn't feeling too happy about being sneered at by somebody I thought had moved far away but who was suddenly right in my backyard.

"We're just riding our ponies," I said. "No law against that, far as I know."

"Don't you give me your smart talk, young lady," Mrs. LaBelle snapped. "Just keep on moving." She opened her purse and pulled out a cigarette. She lit the cigarette, took a deep drag, then closed the purse with a loud click.

I would have kept moving, but her nasty tone had already gotten under my skin. "There *is* a law against littering," I said. "You might want to pick up your cell phone."

I saw Bee's head whip around in shock. If Daddy had heard me say that, he would have grounded me for a week, but he was back in his office in Charleston.

Mrs. LaBelle's eyes narrowed, and all the lines in her face stood out, showing how truly angry she was. For half a second I thought she might actually come over and try to slap me.

"*What* did you just say to me?" she demanded. The words came out in a cold hiss, as if she was having a hard time getting air through her throat.

I stretched my lips and gave her the nicest smile I possibly could. "I said, 'I think you dropped your cell phone,' ma'am."

Her eyes flicked to the phone sitting a couple feet away in the dirt and then came back to me. I could tell she was embarrassed because we had seen her throw the phone, and her embarrassment made her even angrier. "You *would* be the one to know about laws, wouldn't you?" she rasped. "You and your trash-talking father."

I could see Bee staring in shock, probably racking her brain to think of some way to make things better, but the situation was already too far gone for her to do much good.

Suddenly I heard the passenger door open and another voice, loud and shrill. "*God*, Mother, at *least* ask them to call somebody who can change the tire!"

Out of the corner of my eye I saw a flash of blond ponytail and a pink bow. Even before I turned, I knew exactly who it was, and my stomach tightened even more.

The girl hadn't focused on our faces yet, because she yelled, "Hey, would you please help—" She stopped dead when her eyes went to my face. "Oh," she said, her voice dripping with dislike, "it's *you*."

"Hi, Donna," I said in a sappy-sweet tone. "I hope you haven't gotten too sweaty and dusty sitting out here waiting for somebody to change your tire."

Nothing about Donna LaBelle had changed. She was dressed in one of her trademark outfits, a pink pleated skirt and lime-green polo shirt. Her skin looked like it had just been washed, right *after* she'd gone to the tanning salon. Her hair was just so, and even from here I could see the gleam of her perfect nail polish. I thought

I might even have seen some of that eye makeup older girls put on. I hated myself for doing it, but I glanced down at my faded riding pants and my chewed nails that always seemed to have dirt stuck under them.

If I'd looked in a mirror, I would have seen the exact opposite of Donna—a girl with sunburn on her freckled face, because she always forgot to put on her sunscreen, and a curly mop of hair that never stayed in place. Fortunately I was wearing a riding helmet, so at least my lack of "Donna-perfect" hair was covered up.

"Sorry to disappoint you," Donna said. She was batting her eyes in a way that told me she was wishing I would drop dead of a painful heart attack at that very moment.

Bee was looking at all three of us as if she couldn't believe what she had gotten herself into. She was walking Buck around the Mercedes, probably hoping I would follow and we could make a quick getaway. When I made no move to follow, she made a last, desperate attempt to make things better. "We can help you change your tire," she offered. "Abbey knows how. Her dad taught her."

"She does *not* know how," Donna said to her mother, as if Bee was an idiot for suggesting it and as if I was way too dumb to possibly know such a thing.

I wanted no part in changing their tire, but there was no way Donna was going to get away with telling me I didn't know how. I jumped off Timmy and walked to the trunk. "It just so happens I *do* know how to change a tire," I said. "I just changed one last week."

That was true, but it was also true that it was the *only* tire I had ever changed, and it was on a small tractor, not on a car. Still, I had learned how to use a jack and how to loosen the lug nuts and how to refasten them again.

I reached inside the trunk and started to pull up the carpeting that covered the bottom, because I was pretty sure that's where I would find the spare tire. I was hoping to find the jack there, too, but before I got the carpet up very far, Mrs. LaBelle rushed over and slapped her hands down on top of it.

"That's okay," she said, blowing her cigarette breath into my face from just a couple inches away. It made me want to gag. "We'll wait."

As Mrs. LaBelle shoved my hands away, she also managed to drop her purse onto the dirt road, where it spilled open. We both bent over to pick it up, causing us to knock our heads together, but it must have hurt her much more than it did me, seeing as how I had my riding helmet on. I straightened up, but not before I caught sight of the small flask that had spilled out along with her cigarettes, lighter, and lipstick.

"Now look what you've done!" Mrs. LaBelle snapped, grabbing for her purse and shoving everything back inside. "Just go away. My husband will be here in a minute."

I stepped back, realizing that her unsteadiness might have been from more than just trying to walk on a dirt road in high heels. Her eyes were glassy, and her lipstick was sort of crooked on one side, like she'd had her head cocked when she'd put it on.

"You heard my mother," Donna said, her voice growing shrill, almost panicked. "Just leave!"

Mrs. LaBelle staggered past me and picked her cell phone out of the dirt. I took a deep breath, getting ready to say something *really* mean to Donna, but when I looked at her again, the words stuck in my throat.

There was so much misery etched in her face that for once in my life I bit my tongue. Donna realized that I had put it all together, her mother's crooked lipstick, her stumbling, and now the flask in her purse. Mrs. LaBelle had been drinking, and Donna knew that I knew.

A wave of something weirdly like sympathy hit me. I hated to feel like that where Donna was concerned, but a voice in my head said it wasn't fair to kick some-body when they were down, not even Donna. I didn't know what else to do. I didn't want to be around them, but we couldn't just ride away. It was getting dark, and even in daylight a person could sit on a dirt road on Leadenwah for hours without seeing another human being. What if Mr. LaBelle didn't get there as soon as they expected? What if he didn't even come? After all, it had sounded like he and Mrs. LaBelle had been hav-ing a pretty big fight on the phone.

I was still trying to decide what to do when I heard an engine and saw a pickup truck approaching that could only have come from Hangman's Bluff. It was moving fast, putting up a big plume of dust, but the driver slowed down when he began to get close and stopped about twenty-five or thirty yards away.

It seemed that whoever was driving was trying to be polite and keep their dust away. Even so, the thick cloud continued to move right past the truck and set-tled over us, coating our tongues and our skin. Mrs. LaBelle brushed her clothes with angry swipes and glared toward the truck.

A man climbed out of the passenger door and came striding toward us. His face wore a stern expression, and right away I recognized Mr. LaBelle. There was no mistaking him, because he was tall and thin with a nose like a hawk's bill and black hair that came to a point and reminded me of Dracula. He wore a pair of cream-colored trousers, a blue blazer, and an open-collared shirt. His shined shoes were already covered in road dust.

He stopped several feet short of Mrs. LaBelle and let out a long sigh. "What's going on?" he asked in a tight voice. "You jerked me away from an important meeting."

"We were coming to pick you up, and I got a flat tire," Mrs. LaBelle said in a tone like it was his fault. "Someone needs to fix it."

Mr. LaBelle didn't say anything, but his shoulders slumped like he was suddenly very tired. I found myself feeling weirdly sorry for him, too, just like I had for Donna. He went around to the trunk, pulled up the carpet, and jerked out the tire and jack.

Mr. LaBelle fit the jack into the side of the car, then glanced toward the truck one time before he stripped off his jacket, threw it across the Mercedes's backseat, and rolled up his shirtsleeves. I expected whoever was driving the truck to come over and help, but the driver stayed behind the wheel with the engine running. The setting sun was glaring off the truck's windshield, so I couldn't see him.

Mr. LaBelle was already starting to sweat through

his shirt as he jacked up the car, but the driver still didn't get out and offer to help. I walked over to where Bee was holding the ponies and swung onto Timmy's back. Mr. LaBelle barely glanced in our direction. We seemed to be beneath his notice, which was fine with me.

I gave Timmy a nudge and started walking him in the direction of the truck. "Where are you going?" Bee whispered, but I ignored her. I had a weird feeling about who was behind the wheel and why he wasn't climbing out. I was getting closer and, with my angle changing and the glare on the windshield becoming less blinding, I could make out the shape of a man behind the wheel. He was sitting, but I thought he looked short and kind of fat. Just like the man who had stolen Yemassee.

I was still about twenty yards away when the man put the truck into reverse and backed quickly down the road until he came to a place where he could turn around. He did a fast K-turn and headed back the way he had come in a big cloud of dust. I watched him disappear with my heart thumping.

Eight

Bee and I trotted without speaking as we hurried to get to the dinner table on time. Dusk was coming on quickly, and the trill of crickets began to echo from the woods along the road. It was a sound I usually loved, but tonight my brain was like a knotted ball of string, full of thoughts about Donna LaBelle, and also about Yemassee and Willie Smalls.

As we started to get close to home, we let the ponies slow down and cool off, and I finally turned to Bee. "I think it was him."

"Who?"

"The man who stole Yemassee, and the man who

got Willie Smalls in trouble and robbed the gas company. He was driving the truck."

"We couldn't see him."

"I saw him."

"His face?"

"Well . . . his shape. He looked short and fat. And
if it wasn't him, why did he stay in the truck and then
back up when I started to get close?"

"Maybe because he had to go someplace?"

"It was him!"

"I know you don't like Mr. LaBelle, but do you
really think he'd hang around with a robber and maybe
a murderer?"

Sometimes Bee was *so* stubborn, but I had to admit
she was probably right. After all, even though I hated
Donna and wanted to believe anything bad that I could
about her, it seemed a pretty big stretch that the father
of a girl I'd gone to school with could hang out with
such bad people. "The LaBelles are some of the biggest
jerks I've ever met," I said as we turned into Reward.

"They seem unhappy."

"Unhappy, snobby, and horrible."

"Their daughter looks miserable."

"She's a jerk. Why are you trying to make me feel
sorry for her?"

Bee smiled. "I think you already feel sorry for her."

I shook my head, unable to deny it. I shot a glance at Bee, amazed as always at her ability to take the high road when all I wanted to do was stomp on people who had made me angry.

"You need to just walk away from people like that and not let them get under your skin," Bee added.

I laughed. "You're just like Daddy. He tells me I've got to learn to control my big mouth."

Bee turned to look at me, her eyes going wide in fake innocence. "Who says you'll ever be able to do *that*? Seems to me your mouth has been out of control ever since I met you."

I was still struggling to think of a comeback when Bee turned to me with a serious expression.

"You aren't going to tell your dad about that guy in the truck, are you?"

"Of course I am."

"What if it wasn't him? If you tell your dad, and Grandma Em finds out, she's gonna ground me for a month. We disobeyed both of them and went looking for Yemassee."

"But we didn't. We just went riding."

"Grandma Em doesn't live in Abbey's World. She's got her own way of looking at things, and she'll be mad as a hornet to even think that we might have gotten close to that man. Your daddy's gonna feel the same."

"I still don't understand why he wouldn't have gotten out and helped. It *had* to be the bad guy," I insisted.

"What if he has only one leg?"

"He doesn't."

"How do you know?"

I felt a stab of resentment that Bee was acting like Daddy and trying to go by cold facts rather than her own instincts. Still, she had a good point about getting in trouble. "We've ridden all over the island and haven't found Yemassee. What're we gonna do?"

Bee shrugged. "Making false accusations and getting grounded won't help Willie Smalls, and it probably means we'll *never* find Yemassee."

I hated to admit it, but Bee was making sense. "So what do we do?"

"We just have to be sure before we say anything. I'm willing to get grounded if we know we're right."

I nodded. "Okay, I won't say anything until we both agree. Deal?"

"Deal." We shook hands.

"So here's another question," I said. "Those guys shot Yemassee with one of those dart guns to get whatever that white thing was, right?"

Bee nodded.

"Okay," I said, " pleased that I was finally catching up to her in the detective-thinking department. "Why did they just happen to have a dart gun in their truck?"

"*Exactly* the question I've been wondering about," Bee said. She let her pony stop and turned to look at me. He immediately dropped his head and started to munch the grass. "What if that wasn't the only robbery those men committed? Remember that armored car?"

I nodded. "They said the guards got drugged."

"The police don't ever say everything. What if they got shot with a dart gun and knocked out? *And* we've been forgetting all about the dead guy. Why did somebody kill him? And who did it?"

I shook my head. "What if it was because he lost his mask in the gas company robbery and he got scared when he saw his face on TV and wanted to give himself up?"

"So you think his fat partner shot him?" Bee asked, her eyes going wide.

"I'm just saying that *could* be what happened," I said. "Unless there's a whole gang and somebody else shot the blond guy."

Bee shook her head. "You couldn't hide a whole gang on this island." She thought for a second. "You think the fat guy might have killed Yemassee once they got her back to wherever they were going?"

I shook my head. "A dog can't talk and give you away. Besides, if they were going to kill her, wouldn't they have done it when they first came after her?"

"I *hope* you're right," Bee said with a shiver.

After we fed and put away the ponies, I ran home to shower and change for dinner at the big house. But to my surprise, when I walked in the kitchen, I found Daddy wearing an apron and holding a baster in his hand. The aroma of roasting chicken hit me right away, and my mouth started watering like crazy.

It was the first time since his accident that he had cooked the way he used to cook, and for just a second it almost seemed as if Daddy's coma and all the other things that happened the previous year had been a bad dream. It made me feel good and warm and safe; it put a huge smile on my face. While Grandma Em's cooking was some of the best in the world, in my opinion, nothing could beat eating a delicious meal in my own house.

Just seconds earlier my brain had been full of puzzling out the connections between the thing in Yemassee's mouth and the men who had stolen her and the dead man and the gas-company robbery, but my surprise at seeing Daddy and the aroma of that chicken drove all that stuff out of my brain. "Boy, am I hungry," I said.

"I'm glad," Daddy said. "But say hello to our visitors."

I looked around to find Mrs. Henrietta Middleton sitting at our kitchen table. I was even more surprised to see Willie Smalls sitting right beside her. Mrs. Middleton was our friend and neighbor, and she was also Deputy Cyrus Middleton's aunt. In addition to that, she and her grandson, Skoogie, had helped save Bee and me from getting eaten by Green Alice, but that's another story. Willie Smalls, of course, was the man Daddy was defending, the man who had been accused of helping out in the Old South Bottled Gas robbery. I had come in the front door and not the back, so I had missed seeing Mrs. Middleton's truck parked behind the house.

"Good evening, Mrs. Middleton," I said with my best Young Southern Lady manners. "Good evening, Mr. Smalls."

I stepped over to the table and shook hands. Mrs. Middleton was a small woman who was bent from all the hardships she had endured. The bones in her hands felt like tiny bird bones, but I could also feel the calluses and the muscles from all the hard work she did in her garden. Her walker stood beside her chair. She needed it because her legs were bad.

Willie Smalls's hands were huge, just like he was. Even sitting down in one of the chairs around our kitchen table, he was taller than me. The skin on his hands was as rough as bark. His fingers wrapped around my hand like a pair of dark mittens, but they were also very gentle. He mumbled a greeting, but I didn't expect any more. He never said much.

Daddy had explained to me a long time earlier that when Willie had been born, his parents hadn't had enough money to go to the hospital. Willie's umbilical cord had gotten wrapped around his neck just when he was coming out, and it had cut off the air to his brain. As a result Willie was one of the kindest and gentlest people you could ever meet, but the brain damage he had suffered meant he couldn't think as well as most other people.

Even as I shook hands, my head was spinning with fresh questions. The last I had heard, Willie was in jail and Daddy was representing him at his hearing. Daddy must have sensed my confusion, because he said, "Mrs. Middleton and I posted bail for Willie. He's going to stay with her until we get all this unpleasantness straightened out."

I glanced back toward Mrs. Middleton and Willie. "He's my cousin," Mrs. Middleton said.

I hadn't known the Smallses and the Middletons were related, but it didn't surprise me, because so many of the people who lived on Leadenwah turned out to be related one way or another. I looked at them both a little closer, because I would have guessed that getting bailed out of jail would be a reason for happiness, but neither of them looked very pleased. Mrs. Middleton's eyes were glassy and sad while Willie hunched with his elbows resting on his knees and popped his knuckles, one by one.

"Stop that, Willie," Mrs. Middleton snapped, after a few seconds. "If you are going to stay in my home, you are going to have to take that confounded habit outside."

"Yes'm, sorry," Willie mumbled. He stopped popping his knuckles, but he kept clenching and unclenching his hands and staring down at the floor.

Mrs. Middleton stood up and grabbed hold of her walker. "Thank you for your advice, Rutledge. We've taken enough of your time. I'll leave you to have dinner with Abbey. Come on, Willie."

Willie stood up and then went over and shook Daddy's hand. "Thank you, sir," he said, then he gave me a wave and followed Mrs. Middleton out the door.

I stood at the door beside Daddy as they climbed into the truck and drove away.

"Willie didn't look as happy as people should look when they just got out of jail," I said.

Daddy looked down at me. "Willie has decided that he needs to plead guilty."

"But . . . you said he didn't steal anything!"

Daddy shook his head. "The only thing Willie is guilty of is drinking on the job with a couple guys who brought a bottle and talked him into it. He's guilty of that and of being a sucker. The problem is that Willie knows that what he did was wrong. He can't under-stand the difference between being guilty of making a dumb mistake and being guilty of being evil."

"What are you going to do?"

"I'm trying to get the charges either reduced or dropped."

"That's good, right?" I asked.

Instead of answering, Daddy just looked down at me and adjusted his glasses so they sat on the end of his nose. It was something he did when he was unhappy with me.

"Those aren't the only charges that need to be dis-cussed," he said.

Daddy turned and walked back into the kitchen without saying another word. What he'd just said and the way he'd just looked at me gave me a bad feeling. I followed him into the kitchen, but rather than saying anything more, his attention was now on the TV. The sound was low, but local news was on, and the weatherman was pointing to a storm off the southeast coast. A name in big letters at the top of the screen said Tropical Storm Dominique. Daddy turned up the sound just as the man said there was a risk it would strengthen to a hurricane.

The announcer said Dominique's movement had stalled due to a high-pressure ridge coming out of the west, but it would probably start moving in another day or so. Whether it would weaken or strengthen, and where and even if it would make landfall, was anybody's guess. He showed a big cone between northern Florida and the Outer Banks of North Carolina, where Dominique would most likely end up. South Carolina, and more particularly the area around Leadenwah, was smack dab in the middle of the cone.

"If this storm suddenly strengthens and heads our way, it isn't going to give us much warning because it's already so close," Daddy said. "Assuming it hasn't died out or turned sharply north, on Saturday morning I'm going to close up our shutters. Then I'm going to help Mrs. Middleton and Grandma Em."

"You'll need my help," I said, thinking Daddy couldn't do the things he used to do all alone.

"I'm able to do more and more every day. I think I can handle that, but while I do the houses, I need you to get the barn secured. Saturday afternoon I've got a van coming to take the horses and ponies inland. Just a precaution, but better safe than sorry, right?"

I nodded. Anyone who lived on a coastal island in South Carolina learned from a young age never to ignore hurricane warnings. As much as I hated to see a storm coming, I remembered the look Daddy had given me a moment earlier and felt relieved that at least he wasn't upset about something I had done.

He turned away from the TV and opened the oven door. Daddy always rubbed his chicken with olive oil then roasted it at a high temperature and basted the skin with the pan juices. It always came out crisp on the outside and juicy in the middle, just the way I loved it. While the chicken was cooking, Daddy put some broccoli in the other oven to roast, and of course we were also having steamed rice.

As he finished with the broccoli, I remembered that

I had asked him to check on any construction projects on Leadenwah Island. "Hey, Daddy," I began. "Did you have a chance to—"

He cut me off by letting the oven door slam closed loud enough to make me jump. At first I wondered if it had been an accident, but he was fixing me with that same dark look he'd had before as he wiped his hands on a kitchen towel. I had a feeling we were going to discuss the "other charges" he'd mentioned.

"I got a phone call just before Mrs. Middleton and Willie arrived," he began.

I felt my stomach tighten but raised my eyebrows, trying for an innocent look. "Yes?"

"Patty LaBelle said you were extremely rude to her and her daughter this afternoon. Is that true?"

I thought about it for a second. "Partly true," I confessed.

"I asked you a yes-or-no question. Either it's true or not true, so which is it?" he demanded.

I thought about telling him that there were times when it would be better not to talk like a lawyer, but I didn't. In the South being rude to another adult, even if that adult was a total jerk, was a crime, and it was even a worse crime if you were a girl. Girls were *always* supposed to be "ladylike." Fortunately Daddy wasn't as ridiculous about that stuff as most other parents were, but he still hated rudeness.

I gave him his hard look right back. "I was rude," I admitted. "But before I was rude, I tried to help Mrs. LaBelle. I offered to change her tire and started to reach into her trunk to get the spare. She told me not to do it and tried to slap my hands away."

I paused for a second, just the way Daddy had taught me in order to get the maximum bang out of what I planned to say next. "Only she dropped her purse, and I saw the liquor flask she keeps in there. Also her lipstick was on crooked, and she staggered a little when she walked."

Daddy didn't react. He just kept looking at me without any expression on his face. It was another of his lawyer tricks. He was thinking that if he just let the silence hang, it would cause any guilt I might be feeling to begin to fester. When I was a little kid, it used to work every single time.

"You still need to be respectful toward adults," he said, after the waiting didn't do any good.

I felt my eyes narrow. "You're the one who always tells me, 'As ye sow so shall ye reap.' I don't think I need to respect somebody just because they've managed to live for a certain number of years. That's not sowing much, is it?"

Daddy's eyes narrowed even more. I could almost hear the wheels turning in his head. After a second he threw a little more kindling on the fire. "You know the LaBelle family has had a hard time. You and I were in that same position not too many months ago. Maybe a little compassion on your part would be appropriate."

Once again I didn't say anything. The silence stretched and soon became a contest of wills. I was not going to be the one who gave in.

"I still don't think you've told me the whole story," he said at last.

I nodded. "Thank you," I said. "I was rude because Mrs. LaBelle was rude first. She said you talk trash."

He raised his eyebrows. "What did you do then?"

"She had thrown her cell phone in the dirt 'cause she was mad, and I told her there were laws against littering." I glanced at the ceiling. "Well, maybe I said that before she called you a trash-talker. I don't really remember."

I could tell that Daddy was doing his best not to smile. He bunched his lips hard and bit down on the insides of his cheeks, but the corners of his mouth still curled upward. Finally he stopped fighting it and gave me a grudging nod. "I know I'm not supposed to tell you this, but good for you."

I thought I was off the hook, but in the next instant

his brows clouded over and he let the other shoe drop. "But we also haven't discussed exactly where you were when you happened to run into the LaBelles."

I took a deep breath and told him the truth, and his eyes got as hard as stones. "I thought I could trust you to make reasonable decisions," he said in a quiet, disappointed voice that hurt worse than a yell. "Clearly I was wrong. Because of your disobedience, you are now grounded. Other than school activities, you may not leave the plantation."

He looked at me and seemed to think. "And one more thing. Because I thought you were growing up, I was giving you the right to make some decisions about certain social activities."

I knew where he was going. I wasn't going to fight him on my grounding, but I would on this. "No," I said, shaking my head. "Please."

Daddy nodded. "Yes," he said in a tone that brooked no argument. "You are going to Cotillion."

"I can't! It's tomorrow night and I don't even have a dress that fits."

Daddy looked at me with a steely glint. "When you make bad choices, you lose other choices. I'll buy you a dress tomorrow. I'm sure you'll love my taste."

We ate dinner at the kitchen table the way we always did during the week, and even though I'd been grounded and was being forced to go to horrible Cotillion, probably in the ugliest dress in the world, Daddy's chicken, roast broccoli, and steamed rice were just as good as they had ever been, and they managed to cheer me up. When we finished, we even had ice cream for dessert, and then in that peaceful time when my stomach was stuffed and I was resting before I went up to start my homework, I remembered the other thing I needed to ask Daddy.

"Remember those plantation journals you showed me one time?" I asked. "The ones you gave to the Historical Society?"

Daddy had been watching a news show on TV and he turned to look at me. "Sure, what about them?"

"Bee and I would like to look at them."

Daddy blinked. "May I know why?"

I explained about the biography we had to write for history and how Bee wanted to write about her earliest ancestors in America.

Daddy's eyebrows went up. "I understand why Bee wants to do this, but I have to warn you, it's going to be a tough experience. You think you can handle it?"

I shrugged. "You've always told me that a person

can't run away from the truth."

He looked at me for a long moment, then nodded. "You're right, but are you really that brave? If you are, you're far braver than I would have been at your age."

"I don't feel brave, but Bee really wants to do this," I said. "I don't think I have a choice."

In truth I was scared of what those journals might say, and even worse, of the way they might say it. I was scared that they might make my best friend decide she wanted nothing to do with me.

Nine

I woke up the next morning with so much anxiety about the plantation journals that I had an upset stomach and barely touched my breakfast. Once I got to school, I realized that yet again I had forgotten to ask Daddy if he'd had a chance to find out about new construction on Sinner's Point, and I wondered when I would be able to do it.

It was Friday, and that afternoon my middle school tennis team had our first match against one of the local public schools. Since Miss Walker's was the only girls' school in the city, we had to play all our matches against coed teams. I played number two singles on our team ladder, and that afternoon I was matched against a boy a year older than me.

He was taller and stronger, but I had already figured out that if boys thought a girl might beat them they tended to get angry and hit the ball way too hard. This usually led to a lot of missed points, so my strategy was to hang in there and look for a chance to give this guy a scare.

I managed to break his serve in the first set, and just like I hoped, he got mad. From then on he began smashing his racket against the fence every time he made a bad shot and hitting the balls so hard that most of them sailed out of bounds. I just concentrated on getting the ball back in the court and letting my red-faced opponent go down in flames as he made all the mistakes.

I was pretty beat by the end of my match, but our coach came over and asked if I would also play a doubles match because two of our other players had called in sick. I said yes, but when I walked onto the court and saw Donna LaBelle on the other side of the net, I realized my mistake. I skidded to a stop and looked for an escape, my first instinct being to go back to my coach and ask her to put me in a different match. Unfortunately it was too late because Donna had already spotted me.

She strolled to the net and gave me a nasty smile. "Abbey Force," she said, all fake sweet. "What a surprise to see you again after our pleasant little meeting yesterday."

"You must have a funny idea of pleasant," I said.

"Well, it's going to be pleasant to beat you and your little partner into the ground," Donna said.

"We'll see who beats who into the ground," I shot back. Once she'd opened her big mouth, there was no way I would have played in a different match. I wanted nothing more than to see Donna LaBelle in tears.

I remembered Donna as a decent athlete from when she had gone to Miss Walker's. But I also remembered that she was like a lot of the boys, in the sense that her temper often got in the way, and if she didn't win she was likely to fly into a rage. As I recalled it was *never* Donna's fault when she lost, but always a bad call, a crummy racket, a lousy partner. I stowed all that away as we got ready to warm up.

Donna was wearing a perfectly pressed white tennis skirt and matching shirt. Her blond hair was tied up in a pink ribbon. She looked like she was being paid to model tennis clothes, and that didn't make me like her any better.

My own curly hair probably was a damp mop next to Donna's perfect locks. My white tennis skirt was a little dirty, which was nothing new, because I hadn't had time to run the washing machine and I didn't trust Daddy to wash my white things because he always put his dark stuff in along with them and made them a different color.

To tell the truth, a little dirt never bothered me unless I was around somebody like Donna. Knowing Donna looked like a *Vogue* model while I looked like a mechanic made me even more determined to put her into a total temper tantrum.

Donna's partner, who introduced herself as Zoë, made me feel better because she wore the only goth tennis outfit I had ever seen. She had purple hair, heavy black eye makeup, a black T-shirt with some tie-dye colors swirling around in a big mess, black shorts, knee-high black socks, and black shoes. A line of Band-Aids ran along the side of one nostril, with a couple on top of each ear and one over her eyebrow. They probably covered Zoë's piercings.

My own partner, Mary Louise Gardner, a fellow seventh grader, was a nice girl but a little slow and out of shape. In fact, I was pretty sure there were eighty-year-olds who could move around the tennis court faster than Mary Louise. When she actually managed to get to the ball, her high, loopy shots were like marsh-mallow puffballs.

Whenever Mary Louise hit one of her puffballs short, it was going to give Donna a chance for an easy smash. However, as we warmed up and I saw how weak Donna's partner was, I began to feel better. I even started to think that we had a chance.

We lost the spin. As Zoë got ready to serve, I was thinking about what jerks Donna and her mother had been and how much fun it would be to win this match. In the next moment my brain betrayed me, and I thought about how miserable it would be to have a mother who was drunk in the afternoon and how Donna's father had looked at Mrs. LaBelle like she was some kind of massive disappointment. I remembered what Daddy had said about trying to show Donna a little compassion.

A second later Zoë's first serve came across the net in slow motion, and Mary Louise actually managed to return it for a winner. The first three games went just like that, with Mary Louise and me winning nearly every point and Donna even double faulting a couple times on her serve.

By the time we got to Mary Louise's serve, I was actually starting to feel like I needed to lose a couple points and make Donna and Zoë feel a little better. That was when we got into a longer-than-usual point and Mary Louise hit one of her short lobs. Right away

Donna moved. She let the lob bounce then stepped under the ball, cocked her racket over her shoulder, and prepared to hit an overhead smash.

I was at net, but Donna was aiming into Mary Louise's corner. It was the smart play, because Mary Louise was, as usual, out of position and would never get to the ball. However, at the very last second, Donna shifted, turning her shoulder toward me, and when she blasted her overhead, the ball slammed me in the stomach, stinging like a giant hornet and knocking the air out of my lungs in a big *whoosh*.

I managed to raise my head to find Donna holding her hands over her mouth. "I'm *so* sorry!" she cried. "I *so* didn't mean to do that!"

I forced a smile and pretended I could breathe. I couldn't be sure she had hit me on purpose, and I remembered Daddy's words about giving her the benefit of the doubt. "No problem," I said. "Barely felt it."

I turned to Mary Louise. "Try to keep the lobs a little deeper," I whispered. Then as I took my position on the other side of the court I saw Donna turn her head and look over at the bleachers for a long second.

I followed her eyes and found Mr. LaBelle. His face was set in a scowl, and as I watched he gave her a big nod and a thumbs-up. I felt the blood rush to my face.

I focused back on the game as Mary Louise served. I waited until Donna started to swing, then I darted to the center of the court and volleyed her return for a winner.

With the score 15–15, Zoë got the next serve, and she and Mary Louise hit a few gentle puffballs back and forth until Mary Louise sent another one short.

I watched Donna move in, once again aiming toward Mary Louise's corner. She let the ball bounce, moved beneath it, and just as before, she turned at the last second and fired her smash right at me. The shot came at my face, but I dodged, so it hit my shoulder. It hurt less than the first time, but I knew it was no accident. I was so angry, I could barely see as I charged the net, intending to slug Donna in the nose, definitely *not* a ladylike move.

Donna saw me coming and danced back a few feet. "I am so *sorry*," she said, her voice all fake sugar. "I just don't know how that happened."

"Why don't you come a little closer?" I said in a low growl. "I'll show you what else can happen with a tennis racket."

"I already *said* I'm sorry." Donna turned and started to walk away, but as she did her head swung toward her father. Mr. LaBelle nodded again and gave her another thumbs-up.

Out of the corner of my eye I saw the two coaches watching us. I didn't know if either had seen the first body shot because they were trying to monitor five matches at once, but I could tell they had at least seen the last one.

Donna looked over at them and gave an embarrassed wave. "I hit Abbey by mistake. I feel *so* bad!"

Donna's coach nodded and waved for her to keep playing. My cheeks were flaming as I glanced at my coach, who just gave a scowl and a shrug, as if telling me she knew it wasn't an accident but there was nothing she could do.

I stayed at the net for a few more seconds and struggled to get my anger under control. When the coaches turned away and started to focus on other matches, Donna took a step toward me and said in a voice that only I could hear.

"You think you're such a big shot because your family's been around for a few hundred years, but you're not. In spite of everything your father did to try and ruin us, my father is going to be rich again. I'm going to go to Miss Walker's again next year. You and I will be on the same campus, and I am going to get back at you, Abbey Force. My whole family is going to get back at your family. Also you and your little friend are going to pay for what you did to me and my mother yesterday."

"What are you talking about?" I asked.

"Don't play stupid," Donna hissed, her face contorting. "You *humiliated* us. You know you did, and you meant to!"

I opened my mouth to say something mean, but then I remembered the flask and her mother's crooked lipstick and the way she staggered. Donna was horrified that Bee and I had seen her mother drunk. "Play tennis," I mumbled, and went back to my position.

After the match my coach gave me a ride downtown to Daddy's office. Daddy hadn't been able to watch me play because he was tied up with his load of new cases, and while I normally would have been excited to tell him about how we'd won tonight I had two horrible things on my mind: the plantation journals and Cotillion.

The receptionist buzzed Martha, Daddy's longtime assistant, who came out, gave me a big hug, then stood back and said how much bigger I looked. As Martha and I were talking, Bee came into the office from her soccer game, and then a second later Daddy came out from the back.

"Ready, girls?" he asked as he led us to the door. I

wasn't ready at all, but I smiled and fell in behind Bee as we followed him outside and around the block to the Historical Society. My stomach was already starting to bubble as we walked.

Daddy's friend was waiting for us just inside the doors, and he took us straight down to one of their reading rooms. Ten minutes later Bee and I were sitting at a table with seven or eight very old leather-bound journals in front of us. They were business and personal records of my family, the owners of Reward Plantation, from the time it was first settled in 1672, through to the time it ceased being a working plantation in 1910.

The journals told how my ancestor François Philippe Force acquired his land; how many board feet of timber he had cut to build his first house and slave cabins and barns; how many hammers, saws, and kegs of nails he had bought; how many pounds of seed he had bought to plant his first crops; and of course, how many "Negroes" he had purchased to start the work of clearing his fields, preparing his rice impoundments, and constructing his buildings. He was especially pleased with the fact that his slaves had come from the Windward Coast, the area of Africa where people knew about growing rice.

The journals recounted how François Force's first

crops had been highly profitable, how he had bought more land to add to his holdings, added onto his house, and bought furniture and paintings imported from England. They also recounted how, early on, he had added to his holding of captive humans by purchasing more slaves at the Charleston slave auctions.

The old-fashioned writing was hard to read. It took a long time to figure out some of the words, but there was no mistaking the part that said, *Bought 4 boys and 2 girls—their ages as near as I can judge Lucy=10 years old, Hannibal=9, Billy=7, Peter=12, Priscilla=10, John=8 for £650.* It sounded like he was talking about dogs or horses, and it made me want to get up and run away. But I stayed.

I was reading over Bee's shoulder, and as she read that passage, I saw her hands tighten on the journal. A second later she let out a breath that sounded almost like a sob, and she turned to me.

"Seven- and eight-year-old boys? Ten-year-old girls?" Her expression was a mixture of hurt and disbelief. Her eyes brimmed with tears. "What happened to their parents?"

I shook my head. There was no information about them in the journal; however, I knew the most likely answer was that the parents had been sold to some other plantation owner, or maybe they had died in the ships on the way over from Africa.

"How could people do that to children?" she asked in a soft voice that carried more accusation than a shout.

The question for me was: How could my ancestors have done that to children?

I opened my mouth, but no words came out. My shame felt so heavy that I was surprised I didn't sink right into the floor. I had no more answers than Bee did, because I also wondered how my great-great-great-great-whatever-grandparents had come all the way to America to escape people picking on them for their religion, yet at the same time they made other people into slaves. How did that make sense? I couldn't answer, but I knew those same genes had been passed on down to me. Was it possible that I could have done the same things they had? I didn't think so, but how could I ever be sure?

Afterward we walked back around the corner to Daddy's office. I looked at Bee as we walked and saw that she had her back straight and her chin stuck out as if she were spoiling for a fight. I assumed the person she wanted to fight with was me, and I couldn't blame her a bit.

If we had switched positions at that very moment, I think I would have hated Abbey Force and her whole family. However, Bee was also my best friend, and even though I totally understood how she felt, I didn't want to let this linger between us.

"Bee, I'm really sorry," I said. "I know my family did bad things. It makes me angry and ashamed."

Bee looked at me. "I know you feel that way," she said. "I'm not angry at you."

"What can I do to make things better?"

Bee was quiet for a moment. "Let's write the paper together. You write about your ancestors, and I'll write about mine."

"But we don't know which of those people were your ancestors, do we? We don't really know much about them at all, right?"

"That's the point. They're anonymous, like horses or mules. I want to write about that. It's important."

"That's not really the assignment, is it?"

"I don't care if the teacher gives me an F."

I nodded. "I don't care, either." If the teacher really gave Bee an F, it would probably be the first one she'd ever gotten in her life. Not so in my case, but that didn't really matter. Bee's idea was a good one.

When we walked back into Daddy's office, the

reception desk was empty, and we took the long way around the corridor so that on the way to Daddy's office I could peek inside Custis Pettigrew's office. Custis was Daddy's partner and one of his best friends. He was also a friend of mine.

I stuck my head into the open door. Custis's blue eyes were staring hard at his computer screen, and he was typing away on his keyboard. A lock of his black hair had fallen down over his forehead.

"Hey," I said.

He glanced up, and his face broke into a warm smile. "Hey, yourself. You guys here to see me?"

"I wish," I said with a laugh. I always felt better when I saw Custis. "It's Cotillion night, and I'm being punished. We're here to take showers and put on our stupid dresses."

Custis sat up straight and raised his eyebrows. "Do you feel as strongly as Abbey?" he said to Bee.

She shrugged. "I kind of like dancing."

I glanced at Bee. She already wore a bra. I didn't. She looked good in one of those flouncy dresses. I looked like somebody stuck a boy with moppy hair in an upside-down Dixie cup.

Custis stood up from his desk. He was tall and lean and towered over me, but one of the things that made

us such good friends was that he never talked down
to me in that way that so many adults tend to do with
kids. He walked over and put his hand on my shoulder.
"Sorry to hear you hate it so much. Is it dancing or
boys?"

"Both."

"I'm guessing that will change, but maybe it won't.
Should we go appeal to the barrister to cut you a little
slack?"

The barrister was Daddy. "I would love it, but it's
not going to do any good," I said.

As all three of us started toward Daddy's office,
Custis glanced at me. "Understand you and Bee made a
pretty ugly discovery the other day."

I nodded, and the picture flashed in my head again
of the dead man lying on the stretcher, his skin white
and pasty and raw from where the flies had been eating.
I gave an involuntary shiver. "It was pretty gross."

We got to Daddy's office, but he was on the phone,
so we stood outside until he finished.

Custis glanced at me again. "You're not looking for
Judge Gator's dog anymore, right?"

I shook my head. "You probably know that's why
I'm going to Cotillion," I said.

"Just be careful," he said. "Leadenwah is normally

about the most peaceful place there is, but there's somebody very dangerous running around."

"Bee and I are both grounded."

"Right," he said, like he wasn't buying it. "I also
understand you ran into the LaBelles."

"Boy, you sure are keeping tabs on me."

Custis smiled. "I keep tabs on all the pretty girls in
this town."

I could feel my cheeks start to burn. "Speaking of
keeping tabs, do you know if Mr. LaBelle is maybe trying to build something out at Hangman's Bluff?"

"I don't think it would be David LaBelle. As far
as I know, he's been trying to sell the property. From
what I heard, he pretty much went broke after your dad
blocked his condo project."

"Donna LaBelle says Daddy ruined her family."

"Not true, your dad just made sure the zoning laws
and environmental laws were enforced. It's not his fault
that Mr. LaBelle tried to ignore them."

"Donna says they're going to be rich again."

Custis shook his head. "You seem to know more
about the LaBelles than I do, but I don't know where'd
they'd get the money. Anyway," he said, changing the
subject and nodding at my tennis clothes and Bee's soccer uniform, "did y'all win?"

"Yessir," Bee said.

It was my turn to smile. "Duuhhh. And I beat Donna LaBelle in a doubles match."

"And now you two are about to transform yourselves into visions of loveliness for Cotillion."

I turned at the sound of Daddy's voice to see that he was off the phone and standing in his office holding up a plastic garment bag with two long dresses inside. He also had a menu from a nearby Thai restaurant. My expression shifted to a scowl.

"Do I really have to go?" I asked. "That dress probably doesn't even fit. Isn't there some better way to punish me?" Given a choice, I would rather have gotten branded like a steer than go to Cotillion, the annual Charleston dance for "Young Ladies and Gentlemen." "I played two matches this afternoon. I'm tired. I just want to go home."

Custis raised his eyebrows. "Surely you're not going to spoil your father's attempt to make you into a lady?"

"I thought you were on my side." I made a choking sound. "I *hate* dancing. And I *hate* boys."

Probably if I ever met a boy my age who was like Custis, I might not feel that way, but boys my age were stupid. They smelled bad, and they thought their burps and farts were the funniest things in the world.

My pony was smarter than almost all the boys I had ever met.

"We discussed this last night. You no longer have a choice in this, and you're not going to weasel out of Cotillion this year," Daddy said. He waved the menu. "Tell me what you want to order, and I'll go pick it up while you girls shower."

Daddy was the head partner of his firm, which meant that he had his own bathroom with a shower. Unfortunately it also meant that Bee and I could get cleaned up and dressed there and make it to Cotillion, which we would never have been able to do if we had to go all the way out to Reward after my tennis match.

Twenty minutes later, with our hair dry and combed, Bee and I walked into Daddy's conference room in our long dresses. Daddy had already picked up the food, and he and Custis both clapped when they saw us, and Custis whistled. It made my face get all red again.

"Haven't you ever seen anybody in a dress before?" I snapped, even though I wasn't as annoyed as I pretended to be. To my amazement, the dress Daddy had bought for me fit perfectly, and it might even have been one I would have picked out myself.

"Hardly anyone as lovely as you two," Custis said.

I grabbed the bag of food and pulled out my curry

and satay and kept my head down as I ate. I absolutely *hated* the way Custis could make me blush at the drop of a hat. It made me want to slug him. Someday I was going to do just that.

A half hour later I was standing beside Bee in a line of other girls inside South Carolina Hall. Just like every other girl there, I was wearing my long dress and my ridiculous white gloves, and in the short time we'd been there, things had gone from bad to worse.

Hearing some too loud laughter, I had looked over to find Donna LaBelle in a dress that looked like it must have cost five times more than Bee's and mine put together. Donna had been laughing ever so gaily as she talked to several boys, as if something one of them had said was the funniest thing she had *ever* heard. When she realized I was looking her way, she whispered something to the boys and they both glanced at me and sniggered. I was starting to head over to pay Donna back for her tennis body shots when the lady who ran the Cotillion made us stop whatever we were doing and line up for another dance.

A minute later all the girls were in a long row, waiting for the boys who were lined up across the room to come over and ask us to dance. It wasn't a choice thing.

There were even numbers of boys and girls, and the boys were supposed to walk straight across and dance with whoever was in front of them. I counted down to see which boy matched my place in the line.

Unfortunately it was Arnie Snowdon. As I watched him he slipped a finger into one nostril, rummaged all around, pulled it out, and squinted at whatever he'd discovered.

"Oh, God," I muttered under my breath.

"What?" Bee whispered.

"Arnie Snowdon is going to be my partner, and he's digging for treasure in his nose."

Bee made a soft choking sound. "He find any?"

"'Fraid so."

I watched Arnie as he flicked something on the floor and wiped the finger on his pants then started across the room with the rest of the boys. Was it any wonder why I couldn't stand boys when they did things like that and didn't wash their hands? For once I was actually glad for my stupid white gloves.

The look on Arnie's face told me he wasn't any happier about dancing with me than I was with him. The music started, and I put my hand on his shoulder. His face was full of red zits, which he probably couldn't help, but his hair had a greasy shine and smelled like he hadn't washed it in about three weeks. I was trying to decide how to tell Arnie about the fantastic uses of something called shampoo when he started talking.

"You go to Miss Walker's, right?"

"Yeah."

"Didn't Donna LaBelle used to go there?"

"Yes," I said. "Why?" Hearing Donna's name creeped me out. After the flat tire and the tennis match, she was suddenly like a bad itch that I couldn't get rid of.

Arnie shrugged. "She was outside when I first got here, and I'm just telling you she said a bunch of really nasty stuff about you. It was, like, all she could talk about."

"We've had several unpleasant encounters in the past few days," I told him. The second I spoke I realized how idiotic I sounded, like I was trying to be some kind of phony Southern Lady. It made me mad, and I wondered if Donna was the reason I wasn't even able to talk like myself.

"What happened?" Arnie asked.

"Donna and her mother were rude jerks when my friend and I tried to help them with a flat tire. I called them on it."

Arnie pulled away, blinked at me, then laughed in

surprise. "Donna said you dissed her mom real bad. Isn't she supposed to be, like, the original Ice Queen?"

"She deserved it."

To my surprise Arnie laughed a second time. "I bet her mom *did* deserve it," he said. "If it makes you feel any better, Donna always treats me like dirt."

Maybe if you didn't pick your nose and wipe it on your pants, I wanted to tell him, but I didn't. I actually found myself liking him a little.

"Anyway," Arnie went on, "Donna says your father, like, ruined things for her whole family, but that they're rich again, and they're going to get back at you."

"Don't believe everything Donna says."

As the dance came to an end I stepped back from Arnie and gave him a nice smile. "Thank you," I told him. "And if Donna treats you like dirt, that's her problem, not yours. You're a nice person."

As I walked toward the rest of the girls I glanced back. Arnie was looking at me, and for some reason his face had turned as red as a boiled lobster.

Ten

On Saturday morning I woke up in the dark an hour before my alarm, but thinking I could use the time to get the barn closed up the way Daddy wanted, I got out of bed, pulled on jeans and a T-shirt, then crept down to the kitchen. While Rufus smacked his tail against the wall hoping for an early breakfast, I turned on the television but kept the volume low and listened to the weather forecast while I ate some cereal. I didn't need sound to understand the threat of Dominique. It was still a tropical storm, but it was moving again, and now the TV weather map showed an arrow pointed straight at Leadenwah Island.

Everybody knows hurricanes are scary, but people who live on coastal islands *really* understand. Just your basic tropical storm can mean winds as high as seventy-four miles an hour. When that happens things like lawn chairs and branches start flying around, going as fast as cars on a highway. If they hit you, they can knock you out or worse. When you sit out a tropical storm or a category-one hurricane, which Daddy and I had done a couple times, the rain comes sideways and the wind howls like something huge and dark and evil that is tearing away at your house, ripping off shingles, trying to lift the whole roof, driving water into places where you never had leaks before. If a person wasn't scared when they heard that sound, they didn't have a brain. If a hurricane was going to be more powerful than category one, *everybody* went inland to higher ground and safety.

I knew that Dominique might turn out to be nothing, but the fact that it was sitting right to our east meant it could also get to be a *big something* and then come ashore very quickly. That was why it made sense to take all the precautions and get the horses and ponies off the property and headed west.

I turned off the television, and Rufus and I went out into the yard and headed toward the main plantation drive. The air was humid and only slightly cooled from the day before. The leaves of the live oaks and the Spanish moss hung dead in the unnatural stillness. The birds were quiet, which meant a lot of them had already flown inland, because animals know about storms. I saw stars in the west, but in the east the coming dawn was nothing but the barest smudge of light behind heavy banks of dark clouds.

Rufus didn't seem to care about the storm. He gave a couple of happy barks then chased three wild turkeys out of the soybean field. The turkeys did what they always do and disappeared like magic. One second I could see them, and the next second they were nearly invisible. I couldn't help but wonder what they would do in the storm and how they would survive.

Thinking about the turkeys made me wonder about Yemassee and where she was, whether she had decent shelter, whether her puppies had been born yet. I started to imagine her curled up someplace with a litter of baby Boykin spaniels huddled around her while waters rose and a hurricane lashed and tore at the world. I kept seeing all those horrible images in my head playing over and over.

Bee and I had checked out almost every inch of Leadenwah, but there was one place left where we hadn't looked. The odds were probably lousy, but if I could get most of my work done before sunrise, I might have time to sneak away, take one more look for Yemassee, and still get back in time to help Daddy put the horses and ponies on the trailer. I was already grounded, but when I thought about Yemassee and her puppies trapped in a terrible storm, there wasn't any amount of extra punishment that was going to keep me from looking one last time.

I went into the barn and flicked on the lights, then went around the outside locking down the covers on the stall windows.

When I finished and walked back into the barn, Bee was in the tack room moving all the saddles and bridles to the highest pegs in case we had flooding. "I couldn't sleep," she said. "I woke up thinking about Yemassee."

"Me too."

We worked hard and fast, mucked out the stalls, got everything we could off the floor, and brought in every loose item from outside, like hoses, tools, and wheelbarrows. When we finished, the sun was just barely rising, and even then because of the heavy clouds in the east it looked like twilight.

"You know," I said, saying what had been on my mind the whole time, "I think we have time for a quick ride to the other side of the island. We could take one more look."

"We're grounded. Besides, I need to help Grandma Em."

"We'll be back before they even have their coffee. They'll never even know we left," I countered.

"Abbey—"

"If the storm gets bad, what happens to Yemassee? What if she's had her puppies? What's going to happen to Judge Gator if they all die? He'll be crushed."

Bee let out a frustrated sigh. "This is crazy, and you know it."

I knew she wanted to go as badly as I did. She just needed another push. "It's not crazy. The reason we have to go is that I have *hunches* about all this stuff. Okay? That's what happens when you're a detective, you get hunches."

Bee shook her head. "What hunches?"

"Okay, Mr. LaBelle tried to sneak around the law once already. Donna's been telling people he's going to make a lot of money on something, so I've got a *hunch* that she's talking about Hangman's Bluff. We've seen all the dirt trucks, and then the mean guard threw us out of there, so that gives me another hunch. Also we know there are strangers at Hangman's Bluff, and strangers stole Yemassee. *And,*" I said, holding up a finger, "all that other weird stuff with Willie Smalls and the two robberies is like . . . like salt and pepper on the meat."

Bee rolled her eyes at the last part, but she said, "You really think Yemassee could be there?"

"I don't know, but think about how you're going to feel when that storm comes in. You're going to be thinking about Yemassee and her puppies, and you're going to be feeling really guilty that we didn't try."

We saddled our ponies and rode out the drive, and we were just trotting down the dirt road toward the paved county road when we spotted Mrs. Middleton out in her yard. She was still living in her old trailer while her new house on Felony Bay was being fixed up. She was leaning on her walker and looking up at the eastern sky with a scowl.

"Morning, Mrs. Middleton," we both said.

She looked at us and screwed up her face. "Now what in blazes are y'all doin' out here on your ponies?" she demanded. "Don't y'all know there's a storm comin'?" She looked back and forth between us, and her eyes narrowed. "Your daddy and your grandma know you're out here ridin' around?"

"We already packed up the barn," Bee said. "And we have someplace we need to go. It won't take us very long, and I just checked the weather forecast. They say it's still stalled offshore."

Mrs. Middleton held up her arm. "And these old bones say they wrong. They say it's coming fast and getting worse." Her brow wrinkled, and she looked back and forth between us. "And by the way, *where* do y'all *need* to go?"

I shook my head. "No place really."

"Y'all still looking for that dog?"

I shot Bee a sideways glance to warn her not to say any more.

"I asked you *where* y'all going."

Mrs. Middleton is a little tiny lady and she's old, but when she got that tone, we didn't have any choice. "Hangman's Bluff."

Mrs. Middleton picked up her walker and slapped it down for emphasis. "Y'all stay away from that place!"

She said it like she knew something. Bee and I shared a look. "Why?" Bee asked.

"There's spirits over there, and I think they likely be riled up with all the bad things that's been happening around here. And now with this storm coming, they be even more upset."

"You're kidding, right?" I asked, but Mrs. Middleton didn't look a bit like she was kidding.

"What spirits?" Bee asked.

"From the gallows, child," Mrs. Middleton said. "They used to hang people there." Then she turned her eyes on me. "You don't think there are spirits, girl, you go there sometime—not today, but sometime—and just listen. You tell me what you hear."

"You think people are doing bad things over at Hangman's Bluff?" Bee asked.

Mrs. Middleton shook her head. "I wouldn't know 'bout what's happening there now. They got it all chained off so you can't go in, but probably both of us got people who were hanged there." She nodded. "But what I do know is you girls need to get home. Right now. Don't make me call your daddy and grandma."

On a small place like Leadenwah Island, every old woman acts like your own grandmother some of the time. "Yes, ma'am," we both said.

Mrs. Middleton turned away and started to hobble back toward her house, but then she stopped and looked toward us again. "I know how bad you girls want to find the judge's dog, but y'all stay off that Hangman's Bluff land, hear? I'm not kidding about things not being right over there. Y'all know that some bad things have been happening around here, and the spirits know that, too. They're stirred up, and they're angry. I can feel it."

Eleven

Knowing we couldn't ride to Hangman's Bluff,
Bee and I headed home at a fast trot and put the
ponies in their stalls so we could get them again
quickly when the horse van came. When we walked
back out of the barn and looked at the eastern sky, the
sun was still just a dull blur behind the growing wall of
clouds. Even so, the increasing light showed the clouds
for what they were: green and black and yellow, clouds
that looked like pus, clouds that would kill dogs and
puppies that weren't protected.

The storm was like a cottonmouth or a big mama
gator, something I wanted to stay away from. At the

same time, I kept seeing Yemassee in my head, a brown ball curled around a squirming mass of frightened, hungry puppies.

Bee must have been seeing the same things in her head, because she glanced down at her watch. "It's barely seven o'clock. We can't ride the ponies over there . . . but how long would it take us to kayak to Hangman's Bluff?"

I blinked, not quite believing what I had heard. It took me a second to think about it. "Maybe a half hour."

"So if we hurry, could we get there, maybe find Yemassee, and be back by nine o'clock or a few minutes after?"

I nodded, my eyes going wide as I thought about what she was suggesting. Even though they were getting ready for the storm, both Daddy and Grandma Em would probably sleep a little longer. If we were wrong and they got up early, they would be worried and angry, but I thought again about Yemassee and the puppies and poor Judge Gator if something happened to them. "Yes," I said, doing my best not to think about Grandma Em and Daddy. "And even if that guard and Leaper are watching the gate, they won't be looking for anybody coming by water!"

I held up my hand, and Bee gave me a high five. "I *know* Yemassee is there!" I said. "I feel it in my guts."

I glanced upward at where the wind was starting to tear at the tops of the live oaks. I thought again of Yemassee, locked in a dark shed or tied to a tree, looking at the sky and feeling the coming storm the way animals can feel those things. "We gotta hurry," I said.

Down on the dock, Bee went to get us life vests and paddles while I went to the two-person kayak that lay upside down on racks and slapped the bottom all the way from the bow to the stern. It was a precaution, in case a snake or a big spider had managed to get inside or some wasps had started building a nest.

When nothing hissed or buzzed out or dropped out, I turned over the kayak and carried it to the edge of the dock. It was going to be a tight fit if we had to bring back Yemassee and a litter of pups, but I thought we could make enough room down by our feet to fit the dogs. Bee had pulled out life vests and paddles from the equipment chest, and we both zipped into vests and chose a paddle. Just before we slipped the kayak into the water, she gave me a look that told me she was having second thoughts.

"What if Grandma Em or your dad wake up early

and come looking for us?"

I was working to smother the same guilty thoughts. "Which is worse," I said, "maybe scaring them or letting Yemassee die?"

Bee nodded. "I guess when you put it that way . . ."

We lowered the kayak into the river. I steadied it to the dock while Bee climbed into the bow seat, and then she held us in place as I slid into the stern.

The tide was coming in, moving in the right direction so it would help us make a fast paddle out to Hangman's Bluff. That was a good thing, because the day was starting to feel different, as if the air pressure was changing and something big and ugly was coming at us from behind the trees to the east.

"Ready?" I asked.

Bee nodded, seeming surprisingly certain.

I shoved my guilty feelings down one last time and pushed us out from the dock. Right away the current grabbed the kayak and started to move us upriver. We paddled to add speed as we let the river take us.

Noting the current's speed and the strength of the gusts in the branches of the live oaks, I had an unsettling thought that the storm was already moving toward us and pushing water inland as it started to come ashore. I sure hoped that wasn't the case, but one unmistakable sign of the storm's approach was the absence of shore birds. Herons and ibis would normally be stalking the mudflats while anhingas would be perched on branches that arched out over the water with their black wings stuck out to either side. This morning there wasn't a bird to be seen.

We paddled hard for about twenty minutes and finally came around a bend in the river that gave us our first glimpse of the end of the island. We dug harder on the paddles and swung around the end of Bishop's Point then paddled hard again as we made our way toward Hangman's Bluff on the end of Sinner's Point.

I could feel the current beginning to slacken, and I let out a sigh of relief, taking it as a sign that it hadn't been storm surge after all, and the tide was operating by its usual rules and would soon reverse course and begin to flow back out toward the ocean. Just like it had helped bring us inland, I hoped it would give us a fast paddle back to Reward.

By now we could see Mr. LaBelle's property, where it sat across the bay formed by the two rabbit ears of Bishop's Point and Sinner's Point. From here Hangman's Bluff didn't look like much, certainly nothing that should have been worth putting up big No Trespassing signs and hiring a private guard. A small bluff at the very end gave the land its name, and its shoreline was thick with tangled undergrowth that looked nearly impossible to walk through.

"You think that guard's still on duty?" Bee whispered.

"I bet not," I said, thinking of all the reasons the guard should be long gone. Who would need him there at seven twenty in the morning with a big storm just offshore?

We paddled close to the land then drifted as we tried to spot a place where we could pick our way through the thick mass of bushes, vines, and trees that grew almost on top of one another. As we moved along the bank Bee's hand shot out, pointing at something. "What's that?" she asked as I back-paddled trying to keep us still.

I looked where she had pointed, but I couldn't see anything but more tangled undergrowth. "What?" I asked.

"There's an opening there. Look as far in as you can."

We backed the kayak another couple feet until I spotted what she was talking about, a narrow channel that cut through the trees and vines. It led back to something wooden that was set into the dirt embankment and looked an awful lot like one of the old rice impoundments from colonial times that still dot the banks of low-country rivers.

"It looks like a rice gate," I said. "But that's weird. I'm pretty sure this was never a rice plantation."

Before I could say any more about how it didn't make any sense at all to find a rice gate here, a gust of wind cut across the water and shoved the kayak several feet toward shore. We both glanced up, and there was no question that the ugly clouds that had been offshore were looming much closer. I felt a tremor of anxiety.

"You still want to go ashore?" I asked.

"Yeah."

We nosed the kayak into the narrow cut and found that the water was deep enough to paddle right up to the wooden thing Bee had spotted. To either side I could see the same big mound of dirt running all the way along the shore. I couldn't tell how far it went, because all the trees and vines and undergrowth made it pretty much invisible from the water.

"Is it a rice gate?" Bee whispered as she dug her paddle into the mud and brought the kayak to a halt with the bow just inches from the ancient wood.

"I'm pretty sure."

"What's it do?" she whispered.

"Rice gates were dams people used hundreds of years ago to let freshwater into rice fields," I said. "The slaves brought the knowledge with them from Africa and taught their white masters how to build them. This one looks like it's about to fall apart, but this dirt's been dug up recently, so it doesn't look like it's been here long."

"Why would somebody put it here?"

I shook my head in confusion. "Haven't got a clue."

Without another word, Bee put her paddle across the kayak and boosted herself out of her seat. She put one leg over the side as if she meant to stand up. I think she was expecting the water to be just a couple inches deep, but it was a lot deeper. She stumbled, struggling to keep her balance.

"Thanks for the warning," I whispered, using my paddle to keep us from getting swamped.

Bee turned, almost up to her waist in water, apparently not even caring that her new running shoes were probably filling up with black, gooey pluff mud. Any other situation and she would have been trying to dive back into the kayak. "Come on," she whispered. "We need to find Yemassee and get the heck out of here."

She was right. I glanced at my watch. It was almost seven thirty, and we had agreed to get back by nine. A yellowish pall now covered the entire sky. The wind was coming harder off the water, kicking up small whitecaps and whistling in the branches of the trees along the shore. Even though the tide would be helping to take us home, the wind was going to be pushing us back upriver. It was going to make the paddling slower and more difficult, especially with a load of dogs.

I climbed out of the kayak, and we pulled it all the way out of the water on one side of the cut so it couldn't drift away while we were looking around.

Bee's legs were dripping mud as she stepped out of the water. She scrabbled up the dirt bank ahead of me, and I could smell the stink of rotting vegetation and dead fish that is pluff mud's signature scent. Bee couldn't have cared less.

She reached the top first, then let out a big gasp and ducked down. "Abbey!" she whispered.

I came up alongside her, staying low so that anyone on the other side of the embankment wouldn't be able to see us. As I peeked over the top I forgot about staying hidden, because the sight that hit my eyes almost made my heart stop.

The huge hole that yawned in front of us seemed to go on forever. It was maybe seven or eight feet deep and probably ten acres in area. The hole was muddy at the bottom but pretty much totally level.

On the far end of the hole two huge mountains of dirt towered over the landscape, and I knew they had to be the stuff that had been dug out of the earth.

"Didn't your dad sue Mr. LaBelle for stuff like this?" Bee asked.

"Yeah," I said, totally confused. "But he's not building anything now. It looks like he's just digging."

"But why would he dig such a big hole?"

"I haven't got a clue."

Beyond the two huge piles of dirt I could see what might have been a shed or barn. But the hole was what drew my eyes. The whole thing was shocking, a horrible scar to the land. Somebody had ripped into a beautiful place and made it as ugly as they possibly could.

Seeing this made me mad as a a momma gator when somebody's threatening her babies. I couldn't wait to tell Daddy and the judge. I didn't know if there were laws about digging holes, but there sure needed to be. What Mr. LaBelle had done here was just wrong.

I knew, from living on a plantation all my life, that topsoil is valuable, and that sometimes people sell it. Low-country island topsoil is more valuable than most because it's so rich, but even so it goes down only a couple feet. But Mr. LaBelle had dug way past the topsoil, all the way into the marl, a thick, junky mixture of clay and mud. Nobody would want marl. It wasn't good for anything, and because of that I couldn't imagine why anybody would go to the trouble to dig such a huge hole.

The shock of seeing the hole had made me forget why we were there for a moment. As my thoughts snapped back, I realized Bee wasn't with me, and then I saw her running along the side of the dirt rim, popping up every few seconds to look at something, then running again.

"Bee, what are you doing?" I said in a loud whisper, but she was already too far away.

I took off, too, but didn't catch her until she'd gone maybe a hundred and fifty yards. We were less than a hundred yards from the end of the hole now, and when I glanced over the top to see what Bee was looking at, I could see the two huge dirt piles up ahead, and I could tell that the shed I had spotted a moment earlier was one of those double-wide trailers. A bulldozer and one of those big trucks that carried the dirt were parked to the left of the double-wide. Bee didn't seem to be looking at any of that but was staring hard across the hole.

I finally managed to grab her. "Stop before you get

us caught," I whispered. We were both panting hard from running through loose dirt. "You see Yemassee?"

When Bee turned to look at me, tight creases cut at the sides of her mouth and around her eyes so that she almost looked like a stranger. It took a second to realize that I was seeing anger—pure, white-hot rage.

I didn't have long to wonder about it, because right then Bee jumped up and started running along the top of the dirt wall.

"Get down!" I hissed, frantically looking around. "Remember that guard and Leaper!"

Bee ignored me. It took a few seconds to catch her again, and I tugged her lower on the bank to get us both out of sight. "Have you lost your mind?"

She turned to me and growled. "Yucca."

"What?"

"There are yucca plants over there. Lots of them. Remember what Professor Washburn showed us? They mark the graves in slave graveyards." Her voice was strained and hoarse as if she had something stuck in her throat.

I crept up and looked over the edge of the embankment and saw the plants that are also known as Spanish bayonets because their leaves are tipped with dagger-like spikes. A bunch of them were growing along the edge of the hole on the far side, not all bunched up, but spaced out like they might have been marking graves. Bee must have eyes like an eagle's to have spotted them from where we started.

"You think those are really graves?"

"Yes."

I wasn't so sure, but having no way to stop her I followed. At the end of the big hole the sides were no longer straight up and down but slanted so equipment could drive in and out. We jumped down and ran across the opening, trying to stay low enough not to be visible to anybody in the double-wide. When we reached the other side, we climbed back up to the top of the embankment and stared down at the yuccas. Some of them had been dug up and shoved around, and pieces of pottery lay scattered on the ground. I knew from the graveyard we'd visited with Professor Washburn that these were definite signs of old slave graves, and walking to the edge of the hole I saw where other yuccas had toppled in and lay in the mud.

Bee came to stand beside me and looked down at the dislodged yuccas. A sound like a growl came from her throat, and then without another word she jumped halfway down and then slid the rest of the way into the hole.

"Bee, stop," I hissed.

Once again ignoring me, she started clawing into the loose packed dirt along the side of the hole with her bare hands. I squatted behind one of the yuccas and tried to spot the guard or Leaper. I saw no sign of them, but even so we had to find Yemassee and get out of there before the storm got worse. The ruined graves were a terrible crime, but we needed to get home alive in order to report it to the police.

I felt a fresh blast of wind and looked up at the sky. The sun was totally hidden now behind the thickening clouds. A glance at my watch showed that it was almost eight. We had only a few minutes before we needed to start back to Reward.

"We gotta go!" I said in a loud whisper.

If Bee heard me, she gave no sign. She kept ripping at the dirt like a dog going after a bone. Her hair was frizzing, and there was dirt and mud on her arms up way past her elbows. I stared at her in amazement, not believing this was the same girl who was always so worried about being neat, keeping her nails perfectly clean and never breaking the rules.

"Bee!"

She kept digging, her eyes fixed on the hole she was widening out. Finally she stopped, and a second later pulled out something that was so totally crusted with dirt that it looked like a rock. She brushed away dirt until the white of bone showed through, and suddenly there was no mistaking the shape. A chill ran from the back of my neck to my feet.

"Please tell me that isn't a human skull," I said.

Bee held it like it was as precious as a bar of gold. "I knew it," she whispered. "I knew it."

When she raised her head and looked at me, tears were running down her cheeks. "This could be someone in my family," she said.

All I could do was nod, because the realization of what she was feeling right then hit me like a sledgehammer.

"These people have to be punished," she said.

"Yeah, but we can't punish them right now. We gotta get out of here," I urged.

Bee looked around, suddenly seeming to see everything else for the first time. "*Why* are they doing all this?"

"I don't know."

Bee kept the skull in her hands, but she turned and started walking toward the dirt ramp at the end of the hole. Rather than trying to stay low and hide, she just headed toward the two huge dirt piles.

I trotted to catch up. "Will you stay out of sight?" I whispered. "We have to find Yemassee and then go. Have you forgotten about the storm?"

Bee spun around. "The storm is what I'm thinking about! Like what five or ten inches of rain are going to do to these graves! They'll be washed away forever."

I stood there, trying to think of some way to get through to her. "I understand how upset you are. I'm upset, too, but we can't do anything about the graves right this second. We'll come back. I promise."

Bee looked at me. Her eyes were wild, but finally she nodded. "Okay," she mumbled, "let's find Yemassee." With that she turned and took off running. I watched her for half a second, realizing with horror that she was too angry to be her normally cautious self, and then I ran to catch her, praying with each step that we weren't about to get eaten by Leaper.

Bee had already come to the first of the huge piles of dirt and started around it, but in the next instant she disappeared completely. I sprinted after her, fearing the worst.

Twelve

The pile of dirt was huge, maybe a couple hundred feet around and thirty or forty feet high. At first glance it looked like a solid circle, but when I reached the spot where Bee had disappeared, I saw that the dirt had been scooped out to form a deep hollow. There was a half-buried truck and a bunch of other junk scattered in that hollow. That's where I found Bee.

"Thank heavens," I whispered. "Can you not run off like that?"

"I saw this opening and thought Yemassee might be here," she said, looking around. "This is weird."

"Where next?" I whispered.

"The other pile," she whispered.

We ran across fifty yards of open ground, reached the other pile, and started around it. I was right on Bee's heels when she slammed on the brakes and turned toward me, her face stretched in panic and silently mouthed the words, *The guard!*

"Where?"

"Over by the shed."

I crept forward enough to peek around the corner of the dirt pile. The man who had chased us off the other day was maybe a hundred yards away. He had a double-barreled shotgun broken across his arm. He wasn't looking in our direction but up at the sky and out toward the water; however, Leaper was just a few feet behind him, and he had his nose in the air like he was sniffing for trouble. It looked like the guard was heading toward the far side of the hole, but I saw the problem right away: if he walked around the hole, he was going to put himself between us and our kayaks, and then, if he did a full loop, he would come back straight toward the dirt piles where we were hiding.

Bee and I started to inch around the side of the dirt pile to stay out of his line of sight. As we rounded the far side we came to a second big hollow similar to the one we had found in the first pile, and we scrambled into it.

"What're we gonna do?" Bee hissed. "He's got us trapped in here. What if we can't get out and the storm gets worse? What if he spots our kayak? What if Leaper smells us?"

"We gotta think." My blood was pulsing in my ears like a bass drum "Okay," I said, trying to shove down the panic that bubbled in my stomach. "You keep checking on where he is, and I'll try to come up with something."

I turned and looked around the hollow, but all I saw was another wrecked truck, hunks of metal all over the ground, and a table made out of a plywood sheet laid over a couple of old barrels. Two masks lay on top of the table, and beside it were some hoses and tanks. I knew it was welding gear because I'd seen the plumber use the same stuff when he had hooked up a new well on the plantation about two years earlier. It wasn't going to help us get away from Leaper.

"Abbey!" Bee hissed. She turned toward me, her eyes wide with fear. "He's changed direction, and he's coming straight at us."

"How far?"

She peeked again. "He's almost here."

Needing any kind of distraction, I grabbed one of the welding masks and heaved it over the top of the dirt mound so it landed someplace on the side away from us. It was a desperate and lame move, but I hoped the guard might hear it and go explore in that direction.

"What the heck was that?" I heard him mutter, his voice sounding way too close for comfort. I prayed he would turn toward the noise and move away from us, but I had no time to worry, because in the next instant a big diesel engine roared to life. Bee and I both froze, and my heart began to *really*, *really* slam against the walls of my chest. The machine was loud and rough, a sound like a bulldozer might make, and the clank of the machine's metal treads grew louder I realized it was coming right toward us.

We were totally trapped, with the guard and Leaper someplace to our left and the bulldozer driver to our right. We couldn't climb over the dirt pile because we'd be visible. I glanced at the wild undergrowth just a few feet from where we hid. It looked impenetrable the way only South Carolina jungle can, an impossibly thick tangle of live oak, pine, and palmetto, interspersed with snarls of honeysuckle; bamboo; big, thorny brambles; wild rose; and plants I couldn't name. There wasn't enough space between the tree trunks, vines, and branches for us to go more than a few feet before we'd be stopped.

The treads continued to grind closer; then they seemed to stop, and for several seconds it sounded like the machine was going back and forth. We could hear the bulldozer blade biting into the dirt right around the corner from where we were hiding.

A second later a huge wall of dirt appeared to our right. The bulldozer was pushing the dirt, and I realized the driver was getting ready to fill in the hollow where Bee and I were standing. We had no choice. We couldn't just wait to get buried alive. We *had* to move.

I had no idea where the guard and Leaper were, but it didn't matter because the bulldozer was just about to push the dirt right on top of us.

"Come on!" I shouted, over the roar of the engine.

I grabbed Bee's arm, and we bolted through the fast-closing opening in the direction of the water. Right away I twisted my head to look for the guard. I saw no sign of him, and for a few seconds my heart soared. We had a clear shot, and all we had to do was run across fifty yards of clear ground then around the sides of the big hole. At the far end we would leap off the embankment, shove the kayak out into the river, and jump in. Once we were out on the water and paddling for home, there was no way they could stop us. We wouldn't have Yemassee, but at least we'd be alive.

We made it across the open ground and began sprinting along the top of the embankment, both of us stumbling in the loose dirt. I saw the river two hundred yards ahead, glinting like dark metal under the overcast sky. My lungs were burning, and I could hear Bee's ragged breathing as she ran just a few steps ahead. She looked like a halfback, with the dirty skull tucked like a football in the crook of one elbow.

We reached the corner and followed the embankment as it turned toward the rice gate and our kayak just below. My heart was beating so hard it felt like it might explode, but we had only a few yards to go.

We neared the rice gate, and as soon as we were above the cut that ran out into the river Bee jumped down, and I followed. The second my feet hit the ground I looked for the kayak, and I heard Bee's intake of breath as she saw the same terrible thing I did.

The kayak was gone. With a feeling of desperation, I looked out at the river and spotted it, low and yellow, floating perhaps fifty yards from shore, turning in a slow circle as the wind pushed it upriver and the tide tried to take it down.

For a second my mind couldn't grasp how the kayak had come loose. We had put it high up on the mudbank, so it should have been impossible for it to blow off and drift free.

My brain was still trying to understand when I heard a very deep growl.

A fresh bolt of fear shot up my spine. I turned my head slowly, barely moving, just how I'd have done it if I just missed stepping on a cottonmouth that was now lying coiled and angry just a few inches from my leg.

Leaper crouched behind us in the shadows, his lips drawn back over his fangs. He was huge, over a hundred pounds of black-and-brown muscle, and his eyes were as cold and as hard as lumps of coal.

The guard stood right behind. He had his shotgun closed and pointed directly at Bee and me. "Well, well," he said with a smile. "If it ain't our two little pony riders." He looked back and forth between us. "What're you girls lookin' for?"

"Nothing," I started to say. "We were just—"

"You've been digging where you shouldn't," Bee said, her voice a harsh rasp.

I turned, giving her a look, wanting to shut her up.

Bee totally ignored me. She still had that mud-encrusted skull in her hands, and now she held it out. "You've destroyed a slave graveyard. It's against the law."

I shook my head, because I couldn't believe she was

saying this. Well, actually I *could*. Bee was an expert at saying all the things you're *never* supposed to say if you're trying to lie your way out of trouble.

"But we won't tell anybody if you pay us some money," I interjected, before Bee ruined things even more. I figured our only chance was to do what the guard would have done if he was in our shoes. I wanted him to think we were as low-down as he was, and that the least troublesome way to handle us was to pay us off and let us go.

The guard looked at me, and his eyes got even smaller. I was pretty sure he was thinking it over. I was "flying in the dark," as Daddy would say, and I put my hands behind my back, crossed my fingers, and wished, praying he wouldn't decide he needed to feed us to Leaper.

The man seemed to think for an awful long time. "How much you want?" he said at last.

"Fifty bucks each," I said quickly.

"I give you fifty bucks each, and you promise to go home and keep your mouths shut?"

"Yes!" I nodded, feeling a flush of relief.

The guy just laughed and shook his head. "Nice try, girlie." He motioned with his shotgun. "Get moving."

"Where are we going?" I asked.

I glanced at Bee, expecting her to look scared to death, but she was just glaring at the guy.

"Lenny'll decide what we do with you."

"Who's Lenny?" I asked, hoping he wasn't the man who had stolen Yemassee.

"He's the one who seen you paddle up here. He told me to wait till you was away from your boat so's you couldn't run away." The guy motioned with his gun again, pointing toward the embankment. "Move." Then he looked at Bee. "Leave the skull."

She shook her head. "No."

"I ain't gonna ask again."

She drew herself up tall. "Shoot me if you want."

I felt a shot of alarm. This guy was not somebody to play games with.

The guy looked at her, his cheeks growing red, but to my surprise he shrugged. "Suit yourself. Just move."

Before I started climbing, I glanced out at the water and our yellow kayak that was nearly out of sight, spinning slowly as it was blown upstream against the current. Now, even if we pulled off some miracle and managed to escape, how would we get home?

I thought about Daddy and Grandma Em. Very soon now they were going to discover that Bee and I were missing and they would start to worry terribly.

It made me feel so bad, I wanted to cry. An hour ago it had seemed like such a good idea to find Yemassee, but now everything had changed and it looked like the worst idea we'd ever had.

"You know," I said, "if we don't show up at home really soon, my dad and her grandma will call the deputy, and they'll come looking. They know we came up this way."

He scowled, but after a second he tipped his head and squinted up at the livid yellow sky and the growing darkness. "Your parents let you come out in that little boat with this storm coming?" He shook his head. "Don't think so."

I thought about running for the water and trying to swim for the kayak, but then I glanced at Leaper. He was still showing several inches of fang, clearly still hoping I would do something stupid.

"Move 'fore Leaper loses patience," the guy barked. "Leaper," he said, snapping his fingers, "you heel 'less they ain't quick enough."

Bee and I scrambled up the dirt embankment while the guard and Leaper came behind us. Sometime in the past couple minutes the wind had kicked up even higher, blowing the loose dirt on top of the embankment so we had to squint to keep it out of our eyes. Overhead the clouds were growing thicker, their colors becoming more bruiselike. I thought about what Mrs. Middleton had said about her bones hurting and the weatherman being wrong, and I wondered if the storm was going to be a whole lot worse than everyone thought.

I didn't have long to wonder because just then the rain cut loose. It came sideways, driven by a wind that had suddenly turned colder and stronger, and it stung our skin, soaking us to the bone in seconds.

One moment we were standing in loose dirt; the next we were in thick mud that sucked at our running shoes. The guard came up beside us with Leaper on his other side, and he tugged the brim of his baseball cap low over his face and hunched his shoulders.

"Move!" he commanded, but the roar of the wind seemed to snatch his voice away. He took a step, but his boot sucked down into the mud and he windmilled his arms to keep his balance.

Bee must have had the same idea, because both of us moved at the same exact time as we turned and shoved the guard toward the edge of the hole. He was already starting to tip, and our shove pushed him into Leaper, and the two of them went over the edge and they half slid, half fell to the bottom.

"Run!" Bee shouted, but I didn't need any

encouragement. With the hole to our left and impenetrable undergrowth to our right, we stayed on top of the embankment, stumbling in slow motion through the mud and the wind and the rain.

The howl of the wind and the loud smack of raindrops on the mud drowned all other sound, so I couldn't hear the guard or Leaper or even the bulldozer engine. With the rain lashing sideways into my eyes, it was all I could do to make sure I didn't tumble off the edge and into the hole. Ahead of me Bee's blurred form slogged and squished through the brown goo.

The rain was cold, and my muscles burned, but I was too frightened to care. I had no idea how we were going to get home. I only knew that we had to get away from the guard and Leaper and the man he had called Lenny.

After what seemed like an eternity, we hit the end of the embankment and ran down onto the cleared earth, where we were able to move much faster. The blurred shapes of the two hills of dirt loomed to our left, and the double-wide and the parked equipment were ahead.

Bee slowed for a second and looked back. "Which way?" she shouted.

I pointed to the right, the way I thought led toward the road.

We started running again. Our feet slapped against the muddy ground, but the sound was covered by the storm. It was almost as dark as night, the rain slashing sideways in driven sheets.

Suddenly, through the blur, a pair of lights appeared. It might have been Lenny, but it also might have been Daddy or Grandma Em or even the police coming to look for us. Maybe they had discovered us missing, and maybe they had talked to Mrs. Middleton and found out that we had wanted to come over here.

We had to take a chance, and I shouted to Bee and waved my arms, running toward the headlights. As we got closer the car angled off toward the double-wide, and just as I was pretty sure the driver ought to be able to see Bee and me, they stopped and honked their horn.

We were only a few steps from the side of the car and maybe ten or fifteen yards from the construction shed. I raced over and slapped my hands on the driver's window just as the door of the double-wide opened.

"Help!" I screamed, and then Bee was beside me screaming the same thing. The driver was a man. There was a woman beside him in the front seat and a girl in the back. They all turned their heads, their eyes wide with fear at the sight of two mud-covered girls slapping on their windows. My heart soared with hope that we were going to be rescued, until I recognized the faces of Mr. LaBelle, Mrs. LaBelle, and Donna.

Thirteen

We stared at one another through the rain-streaked glass. For a few seconds no one spoke or moved; then Mr. LaBelle's attention shifted, and he swung his head toward the man who had come out of the construction shed and was now framed in the headlights.

It was the man who had stolen Yemassee, and as he stared at Bee and me his eyes burned with a glowering anger.

Mr. LaBelle turned and said something to Mrs. LaBelle and Donna. Then he opened the door and climbed out of the car.

"What are you two doing here?" he demanded, a worried edge in his voice. He wasn't wearing a raincoat, just a sport coat and shirt. He was getting soaked, but if he felt it, he didn't seem to care.

I stepped in front of Bee before she could speak. "Our kayak got blown onto your property. We need a ride home right away."

Mr. LaBelle's face relaxed a little. For a second I thought he was going to tell us to get into the car so he could drive us back to Reward, but then I heard yelling behind me.

It was the guard. He was limping, and he and the dog and the shotgun were covered with massive amounts of mud.

"Grab them two, Lenny!" the guy snarled as he got close enough to make himself heard over the storm. "They pushed me and Leaper into the hole!"

"*They* pushed you into the hole?" Lenny said.

"Yeah, they been *lookin' around.*"

That was when Bee chose to step around me and hold out the skull, which the rain had washed clean. "Yeah, and we found the graves you destroyed!"

Mr. LaBelle's eyes went wide, and he threw an alarmed look at Lenny. "What?"

Lenny paid no attention to Mr. LaBelle. He was

glaring at Bee and me with an anger that made fear bubble up inside my belly. I tried to tell myself it was okay because Mr. LaBelle was in charge. He was a jerk, but he wouldn't let anything bad happen to us, not in front of his wife and daughter. If we could keep things from getting any worse, I thought we could still get in his car and drive out of there.

That was when Bee pretty much killed any chance of things not getting worse. "I'm telling the police and everybody who will listen," she shouted. "You're destroying graves. That's against the law, and it's . . . evil."

Her eyes were slits, the skin pulled tight on her face, her hair plastered to her skull, and rain dripping off her nose. She had no thought of trying to get out of there safely. Those graves mattered to her so much that all she cared about was making sure all these men got punished for what they had done.

Mr. LaBelle held up his hands and smiled. When he did that, he seemed so confident and so totally in charge and believable. Daddy had always said Mr. LaBelle was such a good talker that he could sell snow to Eskimos and that was the reason he had been able to get away with breaking so many rules. Of course that was before he ran into Daddy.

"Whoa there, young lady," Mr. LaBelle said. "Those are some pretty serious allegations you're making."

Lenny cleared his throat. "I think we got us a problem, LaBelle," he said. I noticed he hadn't said "Mr. LaBelle," and for some reason that made me nervous.

Bee's chest was heaving and she still had that crazy look in her eyes. Even so, I was praying she might give in and let Mr. LaBelle think he'd had a victory. Then we could get in the car and go home. Please, Bee! I thought.

"We won't really say anything, will we, Bee?" I prodded.

Bee never got a chance to answer, because the guard spoke for a second time, his voice louder than before. "Is anybody listenin'? They was *lookin' around*!"

About that time Mrs. LaBelle opened her door and got out of the car, holding a newspaper over her head. She was soaked in seconds, and her hairdo collapsed like a dead bird. "What is going *on*?" she demanded. "Why are these girls here, and *what* are we waiting for? We need to get off this island!" She glared at her husband. "I don't even know why you *insisted* we come here."

Mr. LaBelle's face had changed again. I couldn't tell what he was thinking, but for the first time since I'd met him, he didn't appear to be in control of what was happening.

"Get back in the car, sweetheart," he said. "I just need to talk to these two gentlemen privately for a moment."

Mrs. LaBelle made an angry sound, but she got in the car and slammed the door. Then Mr. LaBelle turned to Bee and me. "You girls stay here."

Finally he waved Lenny toward the double-wide. "Step over here, please."

Lenny looked at the guard. "You come, too, Possum," he said.

The guard told Leaper to sit, then followed Mr. LaBelle and Lenny to the double-wide. When Mr. LaBelle pulled open the door, I swore I saw a sort of wire pen inside. That could have been where they were holding Yemassee, but at that moment I had a lot more on my mind than her.

As soon as Mr. LaBelle and the two men disappeared inside, I looked at Leaper and thought about trying to make a run for it. I gave up on the idea right away, because Leaper was staring at me like if I moved half an inch, I was going to be dinner.

If we couldn't run, maybe we could get in the LaBelles' car. Once we were inside, we could just flat refuse to get out. I reached for the door handle, but as if she'd been watching me and waiting for me to make exactly that move, Donna's hand shot out and hit the lock button.

"Donna, let us in," I pleaded.

She put her face up close to the window and shook her head.

"Please, it's life and death!"

She gave me a look like she knew I was lying, and her mother wouldn't even look at me.

Before I could say anything else, the double-wide door opened and the three men came out. Right away I knew something was wrong, because Mr. LaBelle walked in front with a sick look on his face and his hands in the air.

Mrs. LaBelle must have caught it right away, because she got out of the car, and this time she didn't even try to keep her hair dry. "Darling? What's going on?" she demanded.

"Shut up, lady," Lenny said. "I'm sure you've heard of corporate reorganizations. Well, we've just had one." His voice was low and gruff. He didn't sound nervous or stupid like Possum. As they came closer I saw that he was aiming a pistol at Mr. LaBelle's back. "Get your daughter out of the car."

"Come on, Lenny, put down the gun," Mr. LaBelle

said. "We can work this out. You're making a big mistake."

"I'll tell you the mistake," Lenny said. "The mistake was not killing those girls the very first time I saw 'em."

Mrs. LaBelle's eyes were as wide as saucers, and her head was swinging back and forth between Lenny and her husband. Confusion etched her face. "David, *what* is going on? Why is that man pointing a gun at you, and why is he making threats?"

"Shut up, ma'am," Possum said.

"You will *not* speak to me in that manner!"

"LaBelle, shut your wife up before I shut her up for you," Lenny snarled.

Mr. LaBelle looked at his wife and held up a calming hand. "Just take it easy, sweetheart. We'll work this out."

Donna LaBelle had gotten out of the car, and she stood there getting soaked, looking at her parents and at Lenny's pistol. "Stop aiming a gun at my father," she demanded. She pointed at Bee and me. "Aim your gun at them! They're trespassing."

"Lenny," Possum said, shaking his head. "I ain't sure I understand. Are we takin' all of 'em prisoner?"

"Whatta you think?"

"Well, I just . . . I think we got us a problem."

"Thanks so much for explainin' that, Possum," Lenny snapped. "All you were s'posed to do was guard the place and make sure nobody came trespassing. It oughtn't to been that tough. Is there anything you can't screw up?"

Donna started to cry, and Mr. LaBelle stepped over and put his arms around her. "It's okay," he said in a soothing voice. "This is just a big misunderstanding."

Lenny let out a nasty laugh. "The mistake was you thinkin' you could throw me and Possum to the wolves."

Mr. LaBelle straightened, gently pushed Donna away, then turned to face Possum. "Don't listen to Lenny. He's just going to get you in deeper. You don't want to go down for murder."

Without seeming to give it a thought, Lenny came up behind Mr. LaBelle and hit him over the head with the butt of his gun. Mr. LaBelle fell to his knees and grabbed his head. There was a little bit of blood leaking out between his fingers and turning pink in the rain as it ran down onto his collar.

Donna and Mrs. LaBelle both screamed, and Lenny pointed his pistol at them and cried, "Shut up, both of you."

I knew, if Daddy was there, he would've said that if an idiot was waving a gun around, the first thing you need to do is get him to stop waving it. "Do what he says," I hissed.

Mrs. LaBelle's face remained frozen in fear, but at least she quieted down. Donna continued to wail, so I walked over, grabbed her shoulders, and shook her hard. "Stop it!"

She looked at me with a shocked expression. I stared hard into her eyes. "You have to be quiet. You understand me?"

Her eyes were unfocused like her brain was someplace else, but she nodded. I glanced at Bee. The crazed anger had left her eyes. From the look on her face, I knew she now understood that if she had kept her mouth shut, there was a good chance none of this would have happened.

Lenny was dangerous and maybe crazy, and from what Mr. LaBelle had said, he intended to kill us. I didn't know why he would do that, or what the huge hole was all about, or how Mr. LaBelle was going to throw him to the wolves. But what I did understand was that bad guys didn't like witnesses, so I thought it was a good bet that Lenny wouldn't risk killing any of us if he didn't have all of us under his control.

That meant the only way to save any of us was for one of us to get away.

I also knew I couldn't count on any of the LaBelles.

Mr. LaBelle was still on his knees. Mrs. LaBelle was trying to help him get to his feet, but she was too much of a wacko to think clearly. As for Donna, she didn't have enough common sense to blow her nose. Which meant hatching an escape plan was going to be up to Bee and me.

I also realized we didn't have much time, because Lenny leaned down and gave Mr. LaBelle a slap. "Get up and get moving." He pointed vaguely in the direction of the big dirt piles. "Take all of 'em over yonder, Possum."

My brain was working overtime. I was thinking that people *just don't* do this kind of stuff, not for real. Part of my brain was convinced this whole thing was just a plan to scare the bejesus out of us, but then I felt a big blast of doubt when I glanced at Possum and saw him lick his lips. Fear sparked in his eyes, and it seemed like he didn't want any part of what was about to happen next. Which meant, unless he was a lot better actor than I was giving him credit for, we were in seriously bad trouble.

"Over yonder, where?" Possum asked.

"Over by where we dug out the dirt pile. Where do you think?" Lenny snapped.

"What're you gonna be doin'?"

Lenny pointed toward the LaBelles' Mercedes. "Gettin' this here car outta sight."

Possum scowled but did what Lenny told him, waving his shotgun, silently telling us to walk. We went in a slow line, with Bee and me in front and the LaBelles behind. Donna was sobbing like a baby, but at least she wasn't making much noise. Mrs. LaBelle was helping her husband walk, and Mr. LaBelle was stumbling and still looking pretty dazed.

The wind was coming hard from the east, hitting our backs as we walked. The rain continued to sheet down, coming so fast the ground was one shallow puddle.

Possum walked a few feet off to the side with Leaper at his heels. He didn't seem worried that any of us would try to escape—not too surprising, since he had a shotgun and a hundred-pound killer dog, and his strongest prisoner could barely walk.

For the past couple minutes, I had been trying to analyze all the angles. It seemed totally crazy to go shooting people just to cover up the fact that they'd dug up some old graves. I mean, that was bad, but nowhere nearly as bad as murder. But if Lenny was as crazy as I suspected, then he wasn't using his head, he was just reacting. Problem was, all my thinking hadn't gotten me anyplace except walking toward what I was starting to suspect was going to be my grave. I decided that now was the time to chuck thinking out the window.

I turned and looked at Possum. I was as scared as I had ever been in my life, but I couldn't let fear choke off my words. Right at that moment talking was the only thing that could save us.

"What was the blond guy's name?" I asked.

Possum gave me a sharp look. "Who?"

"The guy whose face was on TV after the gas-company robbery."

"Name was Jimbo."

"You know Lenny killed him, right?" Of course I didn't know for absolute certain that Lenny had killed Jimbo, but I was also pretty sure it was the right guess.

"No, he didn't."

"Did so. We found the body."

"No. Jimbo quit."

"Lenny tell you that?"

"Yeah, he said Jimbo got scared when his face was on TV and he lit out."

"He may have tried to quit, but Lenny killed him. I'm sure it's been on TV."

"We ain't got no TV since Jimbo left. Lenny got mad and shot it."

"He probably shot it so you couldn't see the news."

Possum looked unsure, but he just gestured with his shotgun. "No more talk. Just keep walkin'."

I didn't move. "Lenny killed Jimbo, and once he's killed all of us, you think that's the end? Why do you think he's gonna let you live? You're his last witness."

Hearing this Mrs. LaBelle began to whimper, and Donna started to sob louder. I glanced back at Mr. LaBelle and caught him giving me a strange look.

"Y'all shut up," Possum growled.

"You know Lenny's going to kill you so you can't testify against him. Tell me you know that, mister. Tell me that you're not so stupid that you don't know what Lenny's gonna do."

"Close your trap, girl, or I'm gonna knock you on your butt. I ain't jokin'. Don't make this worse on yourself."

I threw a glance at Bee. Her eyes looked clearer, like she was starting to think as well as she normally did. I felt a small swell of hope.

"What did you do with the dog?" Bee asked Possum.

"What dog?" Possum asked. I could tell that he was rattled, and that gave me a little more hope.

"The Boykin spaniel Jimbo and Lenny stole."

Possum's eyes went toward the double-wide.

"She had her puppies yet?" Bee asked.

He screwed up his face as if he couldn't believe she was stupid enough to ask about puppies when we were a couple minutes away from getting shot.

"Yeah."

"We all know what Lenny's gonna do to us," she said, sounding genuinely terrified. "Would you let us at least see the puppies? Just for a second? Please?"

Possum closed his eyes and swallowed. When he opened them again, he looked miserable. He glanced back, but Lenny had driven the Mercedes somewhere out of sight.

"Please?" Bee said again.

"Please?" I echoed.

"One look," Possum growled. "That's it. No touchin' 'em. Real quick."

"What are you talking about?" Mr. LaBelle mumbled. "Puppies?"

Bee and I ignored him. As we turned toward the double-wide Bee said to Possum, "Thanks, mister. We promise we won't touch 'em."

Bee glanced at me, and I just hoped we were thinking the exact same thing. As we got to the trailer two things had to happen, and they had to happen really, really quick. One of them I couldn't control at all. I just had to hope I got lucky, but in order to get lucky, I had to be standing in the right spot.

We walked up to the trailer and stopped. Possum stepped up close and motioned toward the door. "Go on. Open it."

I stepped on the front step, which consisted of a board set on top of two cinder blocks. I grasped the handle and pulled the door against the wind, which tried to hold it closed. With the door open a crack, I could see Yemassee behind some wire in the far corner, surrounded by a ball of little puppies.

"Go on in and see 'em. That's what you wanted," Possum said.

I shook my head and pretended to pull the door as hard as I could. "I can't get it open."

Possum got up onto the step beside me, grabbed the door, jerked it open, and tried to push me farther inside. I grabbed the doorjamb, causing Possum to take a step past me, up into the double-wide. "They're right in that there corner," he said, pointing.

Leaper did exactly what I had been hoping. Just like any other dog, he was curious about other dogs, so he nosed inside behind Possum. As soon as she saw Leaper, Yemassee let out a warning growl, but I couldn't worry about her yet. Bee gave Possum a shove, and I slammed the door hard behind him.

"What are you doing?" Mr. LaBelle demanded.

"We're running," said Bee, "and you better run, too."

"No, you can't run. They'll shoot us."

I realized he must have had all the sense knocked out of his head when Lenny had hit him, and I looked back at the others. "Run!" I said.

"Why you—" I heard Possum say from the other side of the door.

Instead of running, I signaled to Bee and we reached down and jerked the board step off the cinder blocks. When Possum jerked open the door and stepped out, I knew I'd guessed right. He had the shotgun in one hand and the door handle in the other and he put his foot down, expecting to find the step that wasn't there. He fell onto his face in the mud, and the wind slammed the door shut behind him, locking Leaper inside.

I darted behind him while he was still down and kicked as hard as I could, right up between his legs. Daddy always told me that if I ever needed to do it, I should kick "like a placekicker trying to hit a fifty-yard field goal."

Possum's head shot up out of the mud, like he'd just gotten the biggest surprise of his life, which maybe he had. A second later it seemed like the pain hit, because he made a little high-pitched noise that sounded like air leaking out of a balloon.

Inside the double-wide Leaper was going nuts, barking and scrabbling his claws on the door, but I was pretty sure he couldn't get out. I saw that Bee had already started to run toward the water, but the LaBelles were standing there like statues.

Behind them, through the curtains of rain, I could make out Lenny as he trudged back from hiding the car. He caught sight of us at the same time, and he took out a gun from his belt and started to run.

In the next instant he partly disappeared, because the wind gusted even harder. The rain started coming down like a waterfall, the kind of rain that is so heavy, you can't see more than a few feet.

"Come on!" I said, but the LaBelles still stood there. There was no more time, so I took off as fast as I could in the direction of the river. "I'm right behind you, Bee," I shouted, but my voice was pretty much drowned out by raindrops spattering into the dirt all around me. Rain was streaming in my eyes, nearly blinding me, but up ahead I caught sight of Bee's cloudy shape as she slipped and stumbled on the rain-slicked embankment.

Behind me, so faint I could barely hear it, Lenny was yelling at Possum. "You idiot! Now look what ya done! We can't do anything until we got all of 'em. Those two girls are witnesses!"

"Stop or I'll shoot," he cried a second later.

I knew he meant Bee and me, but he couldn't see us through all the curtains of rain, so I kept going. I didn't have any idea what the LaBelles had done, but I figured they had probably just stood there. I slipped and fell every few yards, but each time I got back up and kept running. When I reached the corner of the embankment, I turned and started toward the rice gate.

I caught the sound of Bee's feet splashing in the mud ahead of me, and then I heard another sound. The rain dampened it, but there was no mistaking a gunshot.

"Stop!" Lenny shouted again, his voice even fainter than before.

"Get down," I shouted to Bee as we both slid down the sides of the embankment.

I heard two more shots, but I didn't care, because the dirt protected us. A second later Bee reached the rice gate and leaped all the way down to the mudbank where we'd beached the kayak. We waded out until the water deepened, then dove in and swam straight out into the river with the rain popping and hissing around us, making the water look like it was boiling. When I got close enough, I saw that Bee had managed to hang on to the skull. She was swimming with it stuffed in the back of her shirt, looking like the Hunchback of Notre Dame.

Fourteen

We headed out from the shore, putting as much distance between Lenny and ourselves as possible. As I looked up- and downstream, the bad news was that there was no sign of our kayak. The good news was that there wasn't any other boat Lenny could use to come after us.

That meant we just needed to stay invisible out here on the water. I was banking on what Lenny had shouted to Possum, namely that they couldn't risk shooting any of us until they captured all of us again. If they killed the LaBelles, Bee and I could identify them as the murderers. That meant if we could keep from getting captured, we just might be able to save the LaBelles as well.

We swam farther into the river, the rain falling around us like layers of gauze. After several seconds I heard something smack the water far off to our left and then something else to our right. At first I was afraid it might be oars, but then I realized it was the splash of fish, and that crazy mullet were jumping out of the water the way they always do, even in a storm.

As we moved out of the bay formed by the two points of land, the wind was whipping the main part of the river into big whitecaps. The waves made it even harder for anyone to see us from shore, but the wind was blowing so much water from the ocean into the river that it was overwhelming the current that should have been sweeping us toward Reward. That meant we were going to have to swim all the way home or go ashore and walk. Either way it was going to take us a very long time.

I thought about Daddy and Grandma Em and knew they must be worried sick by now. Would it even enter their minds that we'd been dumb enough to go out in a kayak? I doubted it. I squeezed my eyes shut, realizing how stupid and wrong and selfish we had been. I wanted to go straight back and beg Daddy's and

Grandma Em's forgiveness, but first we had a whole lot of swimming ahead of us.

We swam steadily for a time, and then we stopped to tread water and catch our breath. I looked up and saw the live oaks waving frantically in the powerful gusts. The wind was coming so hard off the ocean now that I was pretty sure the weatherman had been wrong and Mrs. Middleton's bones had been right. This had to be worse than a tropical storm.

The whitecaps made it hard to take breaths without getting water in our mouths. We were in a rush to get home and warn people about what was happening to the LaBelles, but all we could do was swim and then rest, swim and then rest.

Even so we both grew tired, and our teeth were chattering hard from the cold. On the shore of Bishop's Point, through the swirling curtains of rain, I spotted a dock, and beyond it a large house. Bee saw it, too. "You think we should get out here and try to use their phone?" she asked.

We swam toward shore and looked carefully at the house. "The shutters are closed up tight," I said. "But maybe we could find a way to break in."

"What if Lenny expects us to try something like that?" Bee asked.

"I think we have to risk it," I said, and started toward the dock.

That was when I heard Bee start to make strange sounds. I swung toward her in alarm, afraid she might be in trouble. "What's the matter?" I asked. "You need help?"

She shook her head, and I realized what I had heard were sobs.

"It's all my fault that we're in this trouble. If I'd kept my mouth shut, we might have gotten away, and we and the LaBelles would be okay. I was just so angry about those graves, I couldn't think straight."

"You thought straight, but different," I said, trying to calm her down. "For once in your life, you acted more like me."

Bee nodded. "I was so angry, I didn't care about *anything*. I just wanted to get those people."

"I know, Bee. I understand. The thing is, it's a really bad idea to bawl when you're trying to swim. It's a great way to drown."

She laughed and nodded and managed to stop crying. We started swimming again, breaststroking so we could talk. "What do you think happened to the LaBelles?" Bee asked.

"I'm betting Lenny got them."

She shook her head. "It's crazy what they tried to do to us. I mean, the graves are bad, and they can probably go to jail, but it's nothing like kidnapping or killing people."

"I think Lenny's crazy."

"Yeah." She slapped the water in frustration. "It's going to take us an hour to get home."

"Don't think about that," I said. "Just get to the dock."

We were nearly there when Bee pointed ahead of us. "Look!"

My heart jumped into my mouth, afraid maybe Lenny had managed to find us. I quickly eyeballed the dock and yard but saw nothing.

"What do you see?" I asked.

"Underneath."

I looked again, and this time I spotted something yellow that had drifted between the pilings and become trapped. I felt a surge of hope and let out a whoop. It was our kayak.

We swam around the side of the dock. The kayak appeared to be undamaged, and even better, our life vests and paddles were still inside where we had left them. I pulled the stern out from under the dock and held the kayak in place while Bee climbed the dock's swim ladder, put on her life vest, and slipped into the bow.

Next she held the kayak to the dock while I climbed out and took my place in the stern. We were shivering, our teeth chattering like mad, but we shoved out into the river and began to paddle hard through the curtains of rain. The rest of the trip went much faster as we worked hard on the paddles with our arm muscles burning.

Finally the Reward dock came into sight. The wind was ripping across the water in sharp gusts, and the rain pounded down the way it had for the past hour. Overhead the sky was so dark that it seemed more like dusk than late morning. I had been harboring a vague hope that, regardless of how mad they would be at us, Daddy or Grandma Em would be waiting there, but the dock was deserted.

They had to be so upset that we were missing, and they would be howling mad when we told them what we had done. They could punish us both later—and I had no doubt they would—but for now we needed them to listen to our story about what had happened at Hangman's Bluff.

We pulled the kayak out of the water and stowed it on the dock, tying it down tight so it wouldn't blow off in the wind. We threw the life vests and paddles in the equipment storage locker, then started running toward the big house to tell Grandma Em that we were okay.

Up ahead of us, through the pounding rain, the window shutters were all closed, giving the big house a lonely, deserted look. For half a second I felt a wave of panic that Daddy and Grandma Em had given up on finding us and had evacuated, or that something bad had happened to one of them in the storm and we hadn't been here to help.

Maybe it was my fear, or maybe something else, but I slowed down and Bee slowed, too.

"Look," Bee whispered. "Doesn't Grandma Em always have those curtains open?"

She was pointing to the back kitchen door. It had lace curtains over its glass window, but Grandma Em liked to look outside when she cooked, so the curtains were always wide open. There was no light peeking through any of the closed shutters, so the house had to be dark as a cave inside. Even more reason to keep the curtains open, I thought, yet somebody had pulled them tight over the window.

"Yes," I said, and I grabbed Bee's arm and pulled her to one side, behind the trunk of a huge live oak. "What if Lenny made the LaBelles tell him where we live? What if he came here looking for us, and now he's up there waiting to see if we make it back?"

"Oh, my gosh," she said as she put her hands to her mouth. "That means he's got Grandma Em!" She started toward the porch steps, but I grabbed her again.

"And he's gonna have us again, too, if we make a lot of noise and let him know we're here. However many hostages he's got, we're the only thing keeping them alive."

Bee looked close to panic. I held up my hands to calm her. I was rattled, too, but it didn't matter. We needed to think.

"We can't jump to any conclusions," I said. "Let's sneak around and try to figure out who's inside without letting them know we're here. Then if there is a problem, we can sneak down to my house and get Daddy."

Bee's voice started to crack. "What about your dad?" Bee asked. "He could be in there, too!"

I looked at her, and my mouth dropped. It made perfect sense that if Lenny had found out where Bee lived and if he'd taken Grandma Em prisoner, he'd taken Daddy prisoner, too.

I felt panic and guilt well up inside me, and I tried to shove them down, telling myself we needed to think and make a plan. Bee grabbed my arm and pulled me

along, and we crept as quietly as possible to the far end
of the house, where the old cypress-paneled library
was located. With the shutters all closed, nobody inside
could see us, but we couldn't see inside, either.

We squatted down below the library windows, put
our ears to the clapboards, and held our breath. Even
with my hand over my other ear, all I could hear was
the wind whipping and screaming at the corners of the
house and the rain hissing and spattering on the wet
ground. Inside the house was as quiet as a tomb. Maybe
we had panicked; maybe Grandma Em was with Daddy
down at our house.

We crept around the side and along the front of the
house, moving from room to room as I kept putting my
ear to the clapboards, trying to hear any sounds coming from inside. There was nothing. When we got close
to the far end, I was pretty sure no one was there after
all. I was about to sneak up onto the squeaky, old front
porch and look through the curtains when Bee tapped
me hard on the shoulder.

I swung my head around, and she pointed off
toward the place where Grandma Em liked to park her
car beneath one of the live oaks. Beside it was a pickup
truck that didn't belong to anybody in my family or
Bee's family.

A cold chill went up my spine. It was one of the

trucks we had seen parked at Hangman's Bluff.

Lenny really was here, and Grandma Em and Daddy might be his prisoners. I felt so much guilt and panic and fear that I thought my knees might buckle.

Bee was moving away from the house. She had a strange, empty look on her face, and she was staring down at the ground.

I forced myself to move and went after her. When I finally caught her, I grabbed her arm. "Bee? Don't go zombie on me!" I whispered, worried that she was so cold and wet and overwhelmed by everything that she might collapse. I was right on the edge, myself. I wanted to give up and feel sorry for myself, but there wasn't time.

Bee let out a big breath and looked up at me as if I was annoying her. "I'm not going zombie. I'm *thinking*!"

"Thinking what?"

"We're going to go to your house and see if your dad is there. If he isn't, we have to assume Lenny has both Grandma Em and your dad. We can call the police from your house if the phones are still working, but if they're not, we have to make a plan. One way or another, we're going to get them out of there, Abbey."

In spite of how bad everything seemed, I felt a small surge of hope, because no matter how wet and upset and exhausted she was, Bee's brain was still working. She was smart as a whip and better at figuring out the complicated stuff than I was. If it came to making a plan to rescue Daddy and Grandma Em, Bee's smarts might make all the difference.

With the wind pushing against our backs and the rain hammering us with millions of little pellets, we splashed up the plantation drive toward my house. When we neared it, we moved off the road and into the field. Even though the rain made it hard to see, we were taking no chances in case Lenny or Possum were waiting there.

The shutters were closed tight, just like at the big house, and as we came around the side, I spotted Daddy's car parked near the back door. It looked as if he had left right in the middle of loading the car, because the screen door that led to the kitchen was propped open and sitting on the porch there was a cooler with the top raised.

There was a loud bark. Rufus had been closed up in the Suburban. The windows were all steamy from his breath, and there were paw marks on the windows, as if he had been trying to claw his way out.

Even if I hadn't been sure before, now I was positive

that Daddy wasn't here. He would never have left the screen door open like this or left Rufus shut in the car. Even so, before I let Rufus out, Bee and I crept up to the side of the kitchen and took a long listen. The house was absolutely silent, so after a minute I risked a peek inside.

There were apples and oranges and cans of soda out on the counter beside the refrigerator as if Daddy had been about to load them in the cooler when he'd been interrupted. I imagined that the interruption had been Lenny coming to the door with a gun in his hand. Daddy had probably stuck Rufus inside the Suburban to keep him from biting Lenny and getting shot for his trouble.

I put my hand on the knob of the inside door and was starting to turn it when Bee grabbed my arm.

"What are you doing?" she whispered.

"We have to go inside," I said.

"What if one of them is in there?"

I thought for a moment and then went to the Suburban and let Rufus out. I let him lick my face for a few seconds, and then I grabbed his collar and pulled him toward the back door. He went up on the porch, sniffed the cooler, then wagged his tail like he wanted to be let in.

"They're not here," I told Bee. "Rufus would be growling if they were. Besides, their truck's at the big house. They must have everyone there."

"What if you're wrong?"

"You stay out here in case I am."

Bee rolled her eyes, but she didn't argue. I waited until she was out of sight in the bushes, then I opened the door and let Rufus in ahead of me. I tensed, afraid that any second he'd start barking or that somebody would jump out from around a corner, but nothing happened.

I hurried over, picked up the kitchen phone, and listened, then I went out and waved Bee inside.

"Phone's dead," I told her, when she came inside.

"What are we gonna do?"

"First we need to get dry," I said. "Wait here."

With the shutters all closed, it was dark as a moonless night in the house. I moved by feel from the kitchen to the staircase, listening to the roar of the wind around the roof outside. Up in my bedroom, I went into my closet and got two sets of dry clothes, including some too big sweatpants for Bee and blue jeans for me, and also a couple of towels. Back downstairs I took my rain poncho and one of Daddy's out of a closet, along with two rain hats.

I handed a towel and dry clothes to Bee, and while we dried off and changed, she asked, "What about Judge Gator? Maybe he's still at his house. We should find out before we do anything else."

To tell the truth, finding Daddy gone had put me in a state where I was just about to lose it, and Bee's clear thinking helped me focus. "Good idea."

We went back outside, where the whole of nature seemed to be going insane, but at least we weren't shivering like a couple of drowned rats. The wind screamed and whipped the treetops like a crazy woman waving her hair. The rain came so hard that it stung our skin wherever we weren't covered up. I paused and thought about the distance to Judge Gator's, then I looked inside the Suburban to see if the keys were there. They were gone.

"You think we should ride the ponies?" Bee asked.

Before I could get a word out, another big gust snapped a tree in half with a crack like a cannon shot.

I shook my head. "They're gone. Even if they weren't, they'd panic out here."

Bee nodded. We put Rufus in the house, and then we set off running through the pasture and took the shortcut to Judge Gator's.

Fifteen

We reached Judge Gator's house and went around to the back, because it was out of the wind. I hammered on his kitchen door, but there was no answer, so I tried the latch. It was unlocked just the way it always was, and we walked inside.

First we went to the bottom of the stairs and yelled up, just in case the judge hadn't heard the knocking, but the house was empty. We tried his phone to see if it might be working even though ours wasn't, but it was dead, too.

"Okay," I said. "Judge Gator isn't here. He's probably already left the island because of the storm.

Probably most everybody has."

Bee lowered her head. "The only reason Grandma Em and your dad are still here is us."

"I know, but we can't worry about that now," I said I felt a fresh blast of guilt that left me almost unable to think, and I couldn't let that happen. "We need to get Grandma Em and Daddy out of the house before Lenny does something crazy."

"Like starts shooting." Bee shivered. "But you said it was riskier if we went back there."

"It's not my first choice, but we can't wait for the phones to start working to call the police, we can't get to anyone else's house in this weather, and we can't leave them there. We're their only hope."

"Then we need a plan."

"Got any ideas?" I asked.

"We could always go back to the house and yell and let Lenny know we're alive," Bee suggested. "Maybe he and Possum would come out and try to catch us. Then we could knock them out or something."

I shook my head. "If Lenny knows we're alive, all he's got to do is threaten to shoot Daddy or Grandma Em unless we give ourselves up. If he did that, I'd do whatever he wanted. You would, too."

Bee threw her hands in the air and started pacing

the room. "Then how do we do it?"

"What if we could figure a way to scare them out?"

Bee started nodding. "Okay, but how?"

I ran to the counter, spotted a pen and pad of paper lying by the phone, and brought them back to the kitchen table. I took a couple of deep breaths, trying to push back my guilt and fear. "Let's figure it out."

Over the next ten minutes, we came up with several different plans. They included starting a fire in one end of the big house. disguising our voices and shouting for help, and pretending we were the police. I liked every one. I was chafing to run out and get started on all of them, but Bee insisted that we compare the risks.

I forced myself to sit, and in the end, with each of us doing what we did best, we put together the best plan and then made a list of all the things we would need. I wrote everything down on the sheet of paper just the way Bee wanted. When we finished and reviewed the list, we jumped up and rushed to the back hall closet, where the judge kept a lot of his hunting and fishing gear. We rummaged around and spotted several things: a four-piece fly rod in its tube, a reel, and a day pack. The day pack was filled with fly boxes and fishing lures that I dumped out on the kitchen table. Then we went to the closet where the judge kept his utility stuff and tools. We found duct tape, an X-acto knife with a razor-sharp edge, a tube of fast-drying glue, electrical tape, and a couple of screwdrivers. We took two of the judge's flashlights from under the kitchen counter. Bee tested them to make sure the batteries were fresh. We found an ice pick in a kitchen drawer, and we tossed everything along with the fishing-rod tube and reel into the day pack.

"We also need a candle," Bee said, reading down our list. "And some of those wooden kitchen matches."

I ran into the dining room, pulled a couple candles out of a silver candelabra, then went back to the utility closet and looked for wooden matches. I didn't find any, but I did spot one of those cheap, disposable plastic lighters. "Will this do?" I asked. "Better than matches in the rain."

Bee nodded, checking the list. "Now we need plastic sandwich bags."

I went into the judge's pantry and found some. Following Bee's instructions, I put the candles and lighter in one bag, then squeezed out the air and sealed the bag. I rolled that bag up, put it in the second bag, then squeezed out the air and sealed that one up as well. Bee nodded in satisfaction. Double bagging meant we ought to have dry candles and a working lighter, even in a hurricane.

While I was finding stuff and loading the day pack, Bee took the skull she'd been carrying in both hands and looked at it.

"You okay?" I asked, knowing what those bones meant to her.

Bee gave me a sad smile. "Whoever they were, I know they would have wanted us to bring those guys to justice."

I nodded, because I knew Bee was right. Checking the list again, I went to the refrigerator and found a package of ground beef perfect for what we needed. I took it out and then went upstairs, to the judge's bedroom, and found where he kept his pills on the bedside table.

He had about ten kinds of pills, and I looked through them and found the one called Ambien. It was the same stuff Daddy took on nights when an upcoming trial made it hard for him to sleep. Taking the bottle downstairs, I ground up two of the pills with the handle of a knife then mixed them with the ground beef. I made two nice, big meatballs that we sealed in two more sandwich bags.

I checked the list once more. We were finished in

the house. I prayed we had thought it out right and had everything we were going to need. But how do you really know when it's something you've never tried before?

Bee watched with a worried expression, but she never said a word. I felt a huge rush of gratitude that she was my best friend and that she had the strength to be silent, because if she had voiced the doubts and fears I was feeling, I didn't know if I would have had the guts to do what we had to do next.

A second later Bee and I were at the back door in the judge's kitchen.

"Ready?" I asked.

"Aren't you forgetting one little thing?" Bee said.

I gave her a blank look.

"A note?"

I slapped my forehead, realizing that in my rush I was about to forget the most important thing. The note might be the one that could save us if everything else went wrong. I pulled out a clean sheet of paper from the pad and started to write.

Dear Judge Gator,
The bad men from Hangman's Bluff have
got Daddy and Grandma Em as prisoners in

the big house. Bee and I had to take a bunch
of your stuff, even one of your fishing rods and
a reel. I'm real sorry about that. I promise we
didn't have any choice. We have to save Daddy
and Grandma Em. Please call the police and
please forgive us.

Sincerely,
Abbey and Bee

P.S. We found Yemassee. She's at Hangman's
Bluff, and she's okay. She's also had her pups.

I put the note in the center of the kitchen table, where the judge would see it when he walked back inside, and then I looked at Bee. "Ready?"

She nodded, and I shoved open the door, the wind sucking it outward and nearly jerking the handle out of my hands. We ran out into the hurricane, and Bee helped me push the door shut.

The wind was even stronger than before. It screamed around the corners of the house with a sound like animals in pain. As soon as we stepped out from the shelter of the house wall, it tore at our ponchos with enough force to nearly rip them to shreds. The sky was almost black, even though it was daytime. The rain was coming sideways, so hard that it hurt my cheeks and banged into my eyes, making me almost blind. There was probably an inch of standing water on the ground, and we splashed and slipped as we made our way to the barn.

The barn's front doors were right in the face of the wind. Sliding them open would have let the wind inside where it would have put terrible pressure on the roof, so we ran around to the side and managed to open another door. We stepped in, out of the wind, but the gusts scraped and tore at the roof and the walls like wild beasts trying to get inside.

Over the howls of the hurricane, we could hear the farm animals moving around in their stalls, pacing and kicking and making nervous nickers. The judge had one horse and two mules, all of them ancient. He had adopted them to provide a good home in their old age and keep them from being put down.

Past the stalls and the area where the judge kept his mowers and tractor stood a workbench covered with tools, clamps, paint, and other stuff. It was the other stuff we were after.

I scoured the top of the bench while Bee looked underneath. She spotted a crumbling cardboard box on a lower shelf, pawed inside for a second or two, and came up with a three-foot length of rusty steel chain.

She gave it a good shake. "How 'bout this?" she asked.

"Perfect," I said.

I stuffed the chain into the day pack while Bee checked our list. "We need rope," she said. "How much you think we need?"

"This should be enough," I said, reaching above the bench to grab a coil of thin but strong-looking rope from a hook. It was about fifteen or twenty feet long. I stuffed it into the pack.

"What else?" I asked.

"A piece of wire."

While I rummaged through the toolbox, Bee found another box on the lower shelf and came up with a length of plastic-covered wire. "This work?" she asked.

It had a good stiffness but was also pretty thin. "Good," I said. I wrapped the wire around my left wrist and tucked the ends under so it wouldn't come loose.

"I think we're ready," Bee said, checking our list. I gave her a nod as if I felt confident about our plan. She looked at me, and I could see that she was trying to hide the same fear I was feeling. With that, we nodded at each other and walked out of the barn.

Back outside we tilted our bodies into the wind and slogged along the shortcut back to Reward, then up the drive toward the big house. It didn't seem possible that the wind could have gotten stronger in the time we had been in the barn, but I was pretty sure it had.

I kept one hand gripping the day-pack strap so it didn't blow off, and my other arm up in front of my face to protect my eyes from all the flying debris. At one point a huge branch snapped off a live oak and went sailing past us, about twenty feet to our left. The branch hit the split-rail fence that ran along the drive and broke two of the rails as if they were matchsticks. Another time we heard a massive crack off in the woods, and I knew it had to be another tree snapping under the force of the gale.

"You sure we can do this?" Bee shouted, her words nearly drowned out by the keening wind.

I looked over at her. She was keeping her hands up in front of her face just like I was. Even so I could see how frightened she was.

"I've done it all my life," I shouted, trying to reassure her.

The old coal-chute door had always been a great way for sneaking in and out of the big house when I was playing games or when I didn't want anyone else to see me. The house hadn't been heated with coal for many years, but the coal chute was still there. It was right next to the outside basement door, which was always locked, but the coal door was small and sort of forgotten. I had tried to get Bee to go down it during the summer, but she had refused, telling me she *hated* small, dark spaces.

Now I saw her shudder at the idea. "I don't know."

"You can do it," I insisted.

She hunched her shoulders and shook her head. "*Exactly* what do we do when we get inside?"

I couldn't blame Bee for asking, but there was just no way to know for sure. It was like a tennis match, where any plans you made about hitting a hard cross court got chucked out the window the moment your opponent hit a drop shot you had to run your head off just to get to.

"First we have to figure out exactly where everybody is," I told her.

"Then what?"

"Then we . . . play it by ear."

"I *hate* playing things by ear."

"I know," I said. "But we're going to save Grandma Em and Daddy. I don't know how exactly, but we're going to do it. Let's not worry about next steps until we know what we're dealing with, okay?"

Bee grumbled something I couldn't hear, but she kept walking.

Ten minutes later we had fought ourselves to the outside of the big house. We slowed down as we got close then took shelter behind a huge live oak. As we gripped the tree's impossibly thick truck, it twisted and bent in the wind.

We paused there, our eyes slitted against the flying sticks and leaves and the incredibly heavy rain. In spite of having put on dry clothes and ponchos, the rain leaked in everywhere, and we were both shivering like crazy. Afraid they would make noise going down the coal chute, we stripped off our ponchos and let them fly away in the gale. In only seconds I was so wet that I didn't even remember what it felt like to be dry.

The house was about twenty-five yards ahead, but barely visible, just the shape of the walls and roof, the dark eyes of the windows where the shutters were all closed tight against the fury of the storm.

In the next second, a crack of light appeared as someone opened the front door, located on the side of the house facing away from the wind. A hooded figure stepped onto the porch, and Bee and I ducked behind the trunk as the person looked out to their left, then turned to the right toward the tree where we were hiding.

After a second the person stepped down off the porch and started around the house. I was pretty sure it was Possum, and I tried to think whether there might be some way to capture him, maybe bonk him over the head. If we could do it, it would leave only one man inside with the prisoners. But that one man was Lenny, and he had a gun. He could kill Daddy or Grandma Em, and he might just do it if he were angry or scared enough or if he thought it was his only way of getting out of this.

I gave up the idea completely when I saw a second dark shape beside Possum. It was Leaper. A thousand butterflies started kicking around in my stomach, but then I noticed something that made me feel a little bit better. Leaper was on a leash. Possum was dragging him, but Leaper had his rear end all hunched like he was scared to death and only wanted to get back inside. Also I knew we were downwind, and there was no way Leaper was going to smell us in this gale.

I nudged Bee, and we crept out from around the tree, back into the teeth of the wind, moving to a spot farther from the house. The temperature was still dropping, and we shivered hard as we squinted through the sheets of rain and watched the man and Leaper make their way slowly down the lawn toward the dock. They were looking for us.

I remembered that we had brought the kayak back onto the dock and lashed it in place. I didn't know if Possum had been down on the dock earlier and if he might notice the extra kayak. If he did, he would know for sure that Bee and I hadn't drowned. The knowledge would be a huge relief for Daddy and Grandma Em, but it would make the rescue much harder.

Possum came to a stop and stared down at the river. Everything was indistinct through the rain, but I could see the seething mass of water, and I could tell it had already risen over the boardwalk that led out to the dock. I wanted to cheer, because there was no way Possum was going to risk going all the way out to where the kayaks were tied.

Sure enough, a few seconds later he turned and started back toward the house. Judging by the way he moved and the way Leaper pulled at his leash, neither of them wanted any part of being out there.

"Should we try it now?" I asked Bee.

"With Leaper?" She nodded. "Go for it."

I reached inside the day pack and pulled out the

two balls of ground beef. Figuring Possum and Leaper would pass within about twenty yards of the live oak where Bee and I were hiding, I lobbed one of the balls to a place where I hoped Leaper would be able to smell it.

I saw the ball splash in the standing water on the lawn, and my heart sank. What if it was so far underwater or the wind was blowing so hard that Leaper couldn't catch the scent? What if the dog wanted to get back in the house too badly to care about food? I couldn't afford to worry about any of that. I threw the second ball, and it landed almost on top of the first.

Possum got closer. The rain was falling so fast that it looked like a solid wall. Possum had his head down, his shoulders hunched forward, as if he was trying to force his way through a waterfall.

Leaper's head was down, too, his stub of a tail jammed as far between his legs as he could manage. He wasn't sniffing anything, just trying to pull his master back to the house. But when he neared the meatball, he paused, then gave a mighty jerk against the leash, causing Possum to stagger sideways a step or two. Leaper sniffed for a half second, then scarfed down the meatballs in two gulps.

Possum snarled a curse and jerked the leash, but he was too late. A second later they were past us, heading into the house, but I was smiling. I was pretty sure Leaper would be snoring hard in about fifteen minutes. I relaxed just a little, but my teeth were chattering so fast I could barely talk. Bee looked as miserable as I felt.

"Ready?" I asked.

She nodded, her arms held tight across her chest as she fought for warmth. We stepped out from around the tree, back into the full force of the gale. The wind blasted us as it came screaming off the river, making me cold all the way to my bones. The only good thing was that there were fewer trees between the house and the river, so there was less flying junk in the air.

We headed to the side of the house where the padlocked cellar door led to the basement, with the old coal-chute door beside it. I got down on my knees and pulled the hatch up. The opening seemed much narrower than I remembered, and it led to a tunnel of pure blackness. I realized it had probably been two years since I last tried to get into the house this way, and I had been a lot smaller. I turned to look at Bee, who was staring at the small opening with a look of horror.

"We have to go in there?" she said. Her teeth chattered as bad as mine, but I suspected it was due to a combination of both cold *and* fear.

I nodded. "I'll go first."

Even as I said it, I prayed I wouldn't get stuck half-way down. I took off the day pack and handed it to Bee and shoved my flashlight deep in my pocket, where it wouldn't bang on anything and make noise. Then I wiggled headfirst into the tiny, dark opening.

Sixteen

The chute descended at a steep angle toward what had once been a coal bin on the basement floor. The space was too tight to do anything but lie flat with my arms stretched overhead and my legs straight out behind me. I couldn't bunch up enough to crawl or squirm, so I used my fingers to pull and my toes to push as I inched downward into the blackness.

Like any house on the coast in South Carolina, the minute I stuck my head into the chute, the basement humidity hit me, filling my nose with wet, stale air that smelled like dog breath. I'm not a chicken about very many things, but breathing that heavy air and feeling almost trapped by the chute walls that seemed to squeeze in on my chest, I started to imagine spiders. Big, hairy spiders. Maybe a banana spider as big as a person's hand. Maybe a black widow or a tarantula. Or a rat.

I'm not a screamer, and I generally *hate* girls who scream every time the tiniest little thing scares them, but by the time I got halfway down the chute, I was picturing the hugest and most horrible spiders and the biggest rats. It was everything I could do not to holler.

Somehow I managed to stay quiet and continued to claw and push my way down the chute. After what seemed like about an hour, my hands suddenly found open space. I grabbed the end of the chute and pulled myself a few inches farther, until my arms came free, then my head.

From there I forced myself to slow down, because there was about a three-foot drop to the old coal bin. I needed to be careful so I didn't make much noise. I could still hear the hurricane's wind outside like the roar of a locomotive. The storm was probably making enough ruckus to cover any sound I might make, but Lenny and Possum were likely very jumpy by now, and they would come right away to investigate anything suspicious.

With my body hanging halfway out of the chute, I felt for the sides of the old bin, and when I touched the rough plywood, I pulled myself a little farther out. Years earlier, when I was still small enough to slide down the chute fast, I had put some old bedspreads in the bottom of the coal bin to cushion my fall when I came shooting out. The bedspreads were still there, all damp and gross-smelling and moldy, but I could count on them to break my fall to the ground. What I worried about was my legs, now much longer, crashing into the bin with a loud thump.

Holding the sides, I pulled myself forward until my knees came out and my legs fell down on the old bedspreads with hardly a sound. I stayed still for several seconds, listening.

Outside the house it sounded like the world was breaking apart, but inside the basement, surrounded by earth on all sides and the weight of the house above, things were remarkably still. Because of that, I could hear other things, like in one part of the house the sound of several different feet tapping the floor or scuffing, while over my head the telltale squeak of the old floorboards as somebody walked through the downstairs. The person's tread was slow and cautious, but they weren't rushing around the way they would have if they had heard me.

I let another moment go by, then put my flashlight into the chute and clicked the light on and off three times, the signal to Bee that the coast was clear. A second later the day pack came shooting down. Then Bee entered the chute, her hands and knees making dull clunks on the metal sides of the shaft.

There was an intake of breath and a curse. Bee's claustrophobia had to be giving her fits in the tight space. I stuck my head back into the chute and shined the light at her.

"Keep your arms straight out in front," I whispered. "Take your time. Once you're close enough, I'll grab your hands and help pull you the rest of the way."

Bee's breathing was hoarse. She had to be so frightened right at that moment. Whatever fear I had felt, Bee was feeling it ten times worse, because she absolutely *hated* tight spaces. The chute had been tight enough on me, and Bee was bigger than I was.

As I stuck my head back into the chute to try to grab her Bee was whispering something so soft that at first I couldn't understand the words. It took several seconds before I realized that she was whispering, "I'm gonna kill her. I'm gonna kill her." I knew she meant me.

It seemed like a long time before her fingers touched mine. Hers were slick with sweat, but I reached up the chute a little farther, grabbed her as well as I could, and gave a big heave. Bee came sliding toward me, and as her head emerged from the chute she took a couple of shuddering breaths.

"You have to be careful not to hit the sides of the bin," I whispered.

"Just get me out of this thing *now*!" she hissed.

"Okay, okay. Just be quiet." With a quick tug, I pulled her the rest of the way. As her legs fell, her heels swung and thumped into the side of the plywood bin. It wouldn't have been so bad, given the noise of the storm outside, but someone had left an empty can balanced on the edge of the bin. I hadn't noticed it before, and when Bee hit it, it clattered to the ground with a loud clang that seemed to echo off the basement walls.

I flicked off my flashlight, and we both froze, crouching in the absolute blackness inside the coal bin. The only thing that broke the silence was a sudden rustling sound, followed by a sharp pain on my right arm. Bee had just swung in the dark and hit me with her fist.

"Don't you *ever* stick me in something like that again," she hissed.

"Be quiet!" I whispered.

I didn't have to say another word, because in the next instant an overhead light went on, momentarily blinding us, and a set of heavy footsteps thumped down the basement stairs.

I grabbed Bee's arm and pulled her against the wall of the bin. Moving as quickly as I dared, I snatched the corner of one of the moldy spreads that padded the inside of the bin floor and pulled it over both of us.

The good thing about the basement was that it was broken up into several different rooms. The main ceiling light was in the first room, right at the bottom of the basement stairs. The light was bright there, but it faded to murky dimness in all the other rooms. There were other lights in each room, but the switches were tucked around corners and not very obvious to someone who didn't know where they were.

Bee and I were in a room that was to the right of the basement steps, and a long slash of bright light spilled in the door. Fortunately the rest of the room, including the coal bin, lay in deep shadow. Even so, if anyone came over to the bin and looked inside, we would be easy to spot. If they stayed a few feet away and didn't shine a flashlight directly on us, I thought we might be okay.

I moved slightly and pressed my eye to the crack

in the bin's corner, where two sheets of plywood came together. There was enough of an opening for me to see out, and I held my breath and watched. My heart was thudding hard in my chest. After a few seconds I let out my breath and took a fresh one, trying not to pant. I kept squeezing Bee's arm.

I tensed as a pair of legs appeared in the bright pool of stairway light. The man, whoever he was, came about halfway down the basement steps and stopped. He was only visible up to his waist, because the ceiling cut off my view of the rest of him. But by the way he was standing, he seemed uncertain about coming any farther. It gave me a flicker of hope. Maybe he would just turn around and go back upstairs.

After a second he came down two more steps and stopped again. I could see him to midchest now. It was Possum. He held a pistol in one hand and a flashlight in the other, and I squeezed Bee's arm harder. He panned the flashlight beam into the corners of the room he was in, aiming the gun wherever he shined the light.

"Leaper," he called out. "Get down here, dog."

My heart went into my throat. What if the sleeping pills hadn't kicked in yet?

"Leaper!" Possum shouted, but the dog did not appear.

"Where's Leaper?" Possum shouted.

"Last I saw he was lying on the dining room floor," Lenny called back, his voice faint, muffled by the wind. "See anything?"

"No," Possum called back.

"What about outside basement stairs? You see any?" Lenny called.

Possum came the rest of the way down. He moved to his left, out of my line of sight, heading toward the laundry room. His footsteps stopped quickly. He hadn't gone all the way into the room but had stopped in the doorway and was probably shining his light around.

After a second he turned, moved across my field of view again, and opened a door. It was the old pantry room, where canned fruits and vegetables were stored and where a big chest freezer held frozen vegetables or game. Once again, from the sound of his footsteps, I knew he had stopped in the entrance.

Finally he stepped into the doorway of the room where Bee and I were hiding. Maybe ten feet to our left, the outside cellar stairs led up to a slanted metal door.

"I see some stairs," Possum shouted. He didn't sound very happy about the discovery.

"Well, check 'em, you idiot. Make sure they're locked and they ain't been opened."

Possum muttered a string of curses about Lenny, what he hoped Lenny would do to himself, and insults about Lenny's mother, but he did as Lenny ordered and started across the room toward the cellar steps.

His feet scuffed along the gritty basement floor, the sound getting closer and closer. I could see him now through the crack, and my heart slammed even harder. If he was curious, I knew it would be easy to walk over those few feet, shine his light into the bin, and see us.

"Blast you, Lenny," Possum was muttering under his breath. "Why ain't *you* the one down in this crummy basement? Why ain't *you* the one pokin' 'round in this dark with the spiders and rats and whatever the heck else lives here? I'll tell you why you don't do it. Y'all're afraid. Any fool with a single bit'a sense would be."

I lost sight of him again as he went right up to the basement doors. He rattled the metal doors hard to make sure they were locked. After that there was no sound. I still couldn't see him, but I was afraid he might start to check other places.

I let go of Bee's arm, reached beneath the bedspreads, and groped around. There had to be something I could use, but for several seconds my fingers found nothing but dust and floor dirt. Finally I touched something hard. It was small and rough—probably an old bit of coal about as big as my little fingernail—but it had enough weight.

Possum's flashlight beam suddenly swung over our way and played over our heads. I froze. He took a step in our direction, but then he pointed the flashlight back at the ground to see where he should put his feet.

I didn't hesitate. The small chunk of coal flew toward the opposite corner, and I prayed that it would hit something. A half second later there was a loud *ding* as it hit a paint can or a hot-water heater or something metal.

Possum sucked in a loud breath and whipped his flashlight beam in the direction of the sound. "What the heck?" he said to himself in a shaky voice. "It's rats. I know it's rats, and I hate rats." With that he turned and hurried across the basement and up the steps.

A second later the overhead light clicked off, and welcome darkness fell over us once again.

Seventeen

When I heard Possum's footsteps on the floorboards overhead and the basement door slammed shut, I let out the breath I had been holding. I could hear Bee also sucking in fresh air. The two of us sounded like we had just run a couple miles. I touched her arm and felt her shaking like a leaf.

"That was way too close," I whispered.

"You can say that again."

It took me a minute to calm down and start thinking again, but I finally remembered the things Possum had muttered and how much he'd hated being down here in the dark. It gave me a glimmer of hope. "I'm thinking our plan might work," I whispered.

Bee let out a long sigh, and I knew I wasn't going to like what she was about to say next. "So here's what I've been thinking," she said. "We need to get some help."

"From who? There *isn't* anybody who can help us. That's why we're down here, right?"

"But we're overlooking something. We don't know exactly who's up there. Don't you think Lenny probably kept all his prisoners together? If he did, that means Mr. LaBelle and his wife and Donna are up there, too."

"So?" I asked.

"We could see if we can get Donna to help us."

"Donna!" I said in a loud whisper. "Are you crazy? She's an idiot!"

"She's also just a kid. It would be easier for her to help us than anyone else up there. Lenny and Possum won't expect it."

I let out a low groan. "You can't be serious. What can she do for us?"

"She can be a distraction."

I gritted my teeth, but Bee was probably right. If Donna was up there, and we could get her to make some noise and be a distraction, it might make all the difference. If we could figure out a way to frighten her, we could pretty much count on the distraction part.

"Actually," Bee added, "she could be more than just a distraction. If we could find a way to communicate with her, maybe she could do more."

"No way. That means we'd have to depend on her to think and have some self-control."

"Maybe I could get through to her."

I thumped my head against the side of the bin a couple times.

"Abbey," Bee said, "Donna *is* a human being."

Maybe, I thought. "Okay, if she's up there, we'll try to get her to help."

"It sounds to me like everyone's in the kitchen. I bet Donna's there, too."

I closed my eyes and tried to picture the square room with the big island in the middle, the stove and refrigerator on one side and the kitchen table on the other. Bee and I had heard the same sounds, the scuff of feet shifting and chairs moving. "You think they're all sitting around the kitchen table?"

"Yes."

"Turn on your flashlight, but keep your hand over the beam," I said as I started to climb out of the bin. "We need to make sure the coast is clear."

She clicked on her light and let just a little bit of light leak through her fingers. Once I was out of the bin, I turned on my flashlight while Bee climbed out. Together we crept into the main basement room and looked up the stairs to make sure the door at the top was shut tight. It was.

"We need a ladder," I whispered, and we went over to the pegboard wall, where Daddy used to hang some of his tools. Grandma Em had hung a stepladder there, just the way Daddy used to. I took the ladder down, and Bee helped me carry it over to a spot we thought was just beneath the kitchen table.

We spread the ladder's legs and clicked the locks into place. We hardly made a sound, but suddenly a set of heavy footsteps thumped across the floor overhead, heading toward the back hallway and the basement door. I turned to look at Bee and tried to think fast, wondering whether we had time to fold up the ladder and race back to the coal bin. We didn't.

I grabbed Bee's arm and started to drag her toward the nearest dark corner when the footsteps halted, turned, and started back in the opposite direction. The turn was followed by a curse, not loud enough for me to make out the words over the screaming of the storm, but enough to recognize Lenny's voice.

He sounded angry and frustrated and maybe even a little nervous. As long as he thought we were alive, though, he wouldn't hurt his prisoners; at least that's what he'd told Possum. I was holding on to that belief like a life preserver, but I knew the more time went by without us showing up, the more likely he'd start thinking we were dead. That meant Bee and I needed to hurry.

Thinking about time brought Judge Gator to mind. Would he come back to his house once the wind started to back off, or would he spend the night in a hotel and come back tomorrow? There was no way to know when he would see our note, which meant Bee and I had to assume we were completely on our own.

We listened to Lenny pace for a few more seconds until finally he skidded out a chair and sat. Bee and I both let out the breaths we'd been holding.

I waited a second to stop my hands from shaking, then pulled the ice pick out of the day pack, climbed the ladder, and began working the pick into the joint between two of the floorboards. Right away dust and bits of wood began falling onto my face, getting into my eyes and nose. I felt a sneeze coming on and clamped my throat shut to keep it from happening.

The kitchen floor was just a few inches above me, and from this close I could hear sounds from the kitchen much more clearly. Someone moved the leg of a chair, and another person cleared their throat. Then came a sound that I never thought I would have wanted to hear: Donna, saying something in a whiny, frightened voice.

I bent down toward Bee and whispered. "It's her! It's Donna."

From the location of the sound, Donna was almost directly overhead. I scratched harder, working the pick farther and farther into the space between the boards. The house was nearly three hundred years old, and the kitchen floorboards, like the ones everywhere else in the house, were originals. Over the years the wood had shrunk and shifted slightly, and in many places there were separations between boards even though almost three centuries' worth of junk had fallen into the spaces and sort of filled them in. The stuff was soft and very crumbly, because it wasn't exactly wood as much as compacted dust and dirt and kitchen sweeping that had been packed deep enough into the joints to almost become part of the floor.

There was now a long slash of light coming through the separation that had opened up when the last chunk fell out. I tried to look through the opening, but it was too narrow for me to make out much more than shadows. The light was yellow and wavy, and I realized

Lenny and Possum must have had a bunch of Grandma Em's candles burning around the kitchen.

I kept scratching, digging even harder, and then at one point a chair scraped against the floorboards and someone said, "What's that sound?"

I stopped scratching and backed down the steps, getting ready to fold the ladder, hang it back on the wall, then run and hide. Before I could do any of that, Bee grabbed the ice pick from my hand and climbed the ladder. She started to make random scratching sounds on the boards.

"What are you doing?" I whispered. "They heard me!"

Bee looked down and nodded. I could see her dim outline in the light that came through the floor and made the basement just a half shade lighter than pure dark. "If you stop scratching, they'll think it's something besides a mouse, maybe a person."

She was absolutely right, and I felt a wash of gratitude. Bee scratched, then stopped and then started again, sounding just like a real mouse, but also making the opening bigger.

Suddenly we heard Possum's voice. He was louder than the others, as if he was down on his hands and knees looking at the floorboards up close. "It's rats," he said. "Same one that knocked that can on the floor earlier. I ain't goin' down there."

"You are if I say you are," Lenny shot back.

I held my breath, and Bee climbed off the ladder as we waited to see if Lenny would order Possum to the basement. Seconds ticked by, then a minute. Finally I breathed another huge sigh of relief. Bee went back up. The crack was even bigger now, and she put her eye to it and held it there.

"I can see Donna's leg," she whispered. "Right above us."

"Close?" I asked.

Bee nodded.

I felt for the wire I'd wound around my wrist, and I started to straighten it.

"You really think we should do this? I thought we were going to get her to help us."

"We are," I said, "but we have to follow our plan, so first I'm gonna poke her."

Bee shook her head. "It's like sticking a pin in a mule's butt. We have no idea what will happen."

"Sure we do. A mule would kick, and Donna will scream her head off. We just have to have everything else ready."

Bee came down the ladder looking as scared as I

felt. Our plan had made sense when we made it back at the judge's house. Only now, thinking about all the things we had to do and how perfectly we had to do them, it seemed pretty much impossible. I gritted my teeth, refusing to think about failure, because there are times when a person just has to stop worrying and get the job done. We would get ready; then we would stick the pin in the mule's butt and see what happened.

Bee must have decided the same thing, because she stepped over to the coal bin and pulled out the skull from our day pack. She laid it carefully at her feet, then took out the fishing-rod case, the candle, the chain, the lighter, and the glue.

She looked at the stuff on the ground and shook her head. "How did we ever decide this was going to work? Are we *crazy*?"

We carried the items to Daddy's old workbench and, taking care to be quiet, we searched through a pile of old scrap lumber for a small piece of board. We found one about five inches long and maybe four inches across. It was perfect.

Doing everything the way we'd planned at the judge's, we measured the candle, then used the X-acto knife to cut it to the right length. I put a big dab of glue on the bottom of the candle, and we glued it onto one end of the board. It dried fast, and a second later we glued the skull on the board so the candle stuck up inside it.

Bee looked at the skull and sighed. "I hope this isn't wrong."

"You're the one who said they would want this."

"I know. But this used to be a person. This could have been one of my great-great-great-great-grandparents."

"People give their livers and kidneys away all the time when they die," I said. "Don't you think your great-great-whatever-grandparents would want their old bones to save your grandma's life?"

That seemed to make things easier. Bee nodded. "You're right."

Next I took the fishing rod out of its case and put it together. Then I attached the reel, pulled out a bunch of fishing line, and ran it through the guides. The end of the fly line was about six feet of thin, clear leader that was nearly invisible.

While Bee put one more dab of epoxy on the top of the skull, I lowered the end of the leader and made sure a good bit of it landed in the glue and stayed put.

While we waited for the glue to dry, we started looking for the last thing we needed. It didn't take long. In one corner we found a baseball bat that must have belonged to Bee's little brother. It was one of those things people can't bring themselves to throw away and end up putting in some dark corner and forgetting. I felt kind of weird taking it, but just like the skull, we had no other choice. I was pretty sure that if Bee's little brother was watching us now from Heaven, he'd want us to use his Louisville Slugger.

Everything was in place. We went back over to the workbench and checked the glue. It had only a moment to go, so to keep my nerves from getting too frazzled, I pulled Bee over to the basement stairs and pointed at the third and seventh step. "Careful of them," I whispered. "They squeak."

She nodded.

"Ready?" I whispered, knowing we were both totally petrified about what would come next.

Bee nodded again. "Where should I hide?"

I pointed Bee toward the canning room. "In there," I whispered as I handed her the bat. "Leave the door open a crack so you'll be able to see."

Coming from the canning room would give her the best chance to do what she needed to do. But everything, absolutely *everything*, was going to depend on Lenny being a consistently lazy boss and sending Possum down here alone. I couldn't even let myself think about what would happen if I was wrong about that.

Bee tiptoed over to the closed door of the canning room. She opened it very slowly, taking care to make no noise. The knob squeaked a little bit, and we both tensed. After a few seconds, when we heard nothing from upstairs, Bee stepped inside and pulled the door closed, leaving it open a crack so she could see what was going on outside. I took a huge breath and went back to the stepladder.

I climbed back up on the ladder and looked up through the opening we had scratched in the joint between the floorboards. It was wide enough now so that right above me I could make out several pairs of legs. All of them were facing inward, which meant that the prisoners were seated at the kitchen table, all facing one another.

One set of legs had pants and heavy shoes, and since I didn't recognize the shoes, I was pretty sure they belonged to Mr. LaBelle. Another pair of legs had high heels, and since I'd never seen Grandma Em in high heels, I knew they were Mrs. LaBelle's. Farther away, at the other end of the table, were another pair of men's shoes and pants, and that must have been Daddy. Beside him were legs with slacks and darker ankles that had to be Grandma Em.

Almost right above me, in the most perfect position,

were the legs I was looking for: Nikes and a pair of blue jeans that stopped a few inches above a pair of pale ankles. It was Donna, and the way she was positioned, she was plenty close enough.

I climbed back down off the ladder, stepped over to the workbench, and checked the glue one last time. Then I used the fly line to pick up the skull and made sure the leader held tight. I took the lighter from my pocket and lit the candle. With that done I climbed back on the ladder, took the wire I had straightened out, and put it up through the hole in the floor.

I glanced in Bee's direction. "Ready?"

"Yes," came back a choked whisper.

I closed one eye, aimed my wire upward, and jabbed hard.

Up above came an ear-shattering shriek, then "OhmyGod! OhmyGod! I've been stung! Owww, owww!" Next came a bunch of kicking and stomping and scraping as Donna's legs spazzed and jerked, and she tried to figure out what kind of horrible insect or spider had just stung the bejesus out of her.

In spite of how totally terror-stricken I felt at that moment, I couldn't help but smile as I jumped down off the ladder.

Eighteen

What I did next wasn't exactly silent, but the screaming in the kitchen right above me covered any noise I made. I folded up the ladder and hung it back on the pegboard. Over by the workbench, I looped the chain over my arm, careful not to let it clank, and picked up the fly rod, bringing the tip around until the skull was almost, but not quite, visible to someone standing at the bottom of the basement stairs. Then I waited.

My heart was pounding so hard, I could barely stand. Even with the racket upstairs and the wind howling outside, the thundering of my heart in my chest seemed to echo like jungle drums.

Donna was still screaming and crying and kicking. My little poke had clearly hurt and also scared the pants off of her.

"Calm down, kid," Lenny snarled for the fifth or sixth time, but Donna just ignored him. Finally I heard him snap at Possum.

"Go down there and find out whatever bit her. Kill the freakin' thing."

"What're you talkin' about?" Possum grumbled. "Nothin' bit her from down there."

"Well, somethin' bit her, and she says it's down there. Go kill it, so she shuts up. She's drivin' me nuts with all the screaming."

Heavy steps came toward the basement stairs. "Leaper!" Possum called.

He turned and went toward the dining room. "Leaper, get up, you lazy piece of garbage."

I heard a soft thump, and then the dog whined. "What's wrong with you, dog?" Possum said.

Finally he came toward the basement steps again. The door at the top of the stairs opened, and a second later the overhead light came on. I squinted against the unaccustomed brightness and instinctively took a half step back. The skull bounced a little on the end of the

line, but I steadied the rod and brought the skull back
so it was just outside the spill of light coming through
the doorway. I knew Possum couldn't see me, but
logic didn't matter, because I was scared half out of
my mind.

I counted the steps as he came down, hearing the
two squeaky stairs. He reached the bottom, and his feet
scuffed on the cement floor. I took a breath and held it
and forced myself to wait.

"I hate rats," he muttered under his breath. "Just
leave 'em alone down here and they won't bother
nobody. But no, stupid Lenny can't let 'em be."

He took a couple of deep breaths, sounding almost
as frightened as I was; then he came a step toward me.
He stopped again, and I worried suddenly that he had
spotted shadows thrown by the flickering candlelight
showing through the skull's eyeholes. If that happened,
he might panic and go back—or worse, call Lenny to
come down.

I squeezed my eyes closed and beamed thoughts at
him, telling him to take a couple more steps. He stood
there forever. I didn't dare breathe. The air grew stale in
my lungs and began to burn. I was desperate to exhale,
but I couldn't risk that much noise.

Finally Possum took another step. Then he cursed

under his breath and took another step, then a third. Three steps had been my signal. I pushed the rod forward a couple inches so the skull with the evil light showing through its eyeholes floated out and seemed to hang in the air, staring right at him. At the same time, I dropped the chain and then kicked it to make it clank, and I made a low moaning sound.

Possum did exactly what I hoped. He let out a scream that was a lot more girlie-sounding than I would have thought possible for such a big man. He also started to turn to run back up the basement stairs, but that was when Bee stepped out of the canning room and bashed him over the head with the Louisville Slugger.

The whole time I had been afraid she wouldn't hit him hard enough, but Bee must have been totally juiced, because she gave him a really good whack. The sound was sort of hollow and squishy, like dropping a watermelon on the floor. Possum hit the ground like a sack of potatoes, and his flashlight and pistol clattered away on the cement.

"Possum?" Lenny's voice came down the stairs. "What're you doin'?"

The sound stirred Bee and me into action. Right away we did what we had talked about. I blew out the candle, put the fly rod on the workbench, and hid the skull under a pile of rags. While I was doing that, Bee grabbed Possum's flashlight and gun and put them on the floor by the coal bin.

All that took about ten seconds; then we rushed to where Possum had collapsed. Each of us grabbed one of his ankles, and we started to drag him. Possum felt as heavy as a dead horse. We both pulled as hard as we could and got him moving. His head was cut from where Bee had hit him, and it left a smear of blood on the cement as we dragged him into the deep shadows over by his flashlight and gun. Tiptoeing as fast as we could, we hurried back to the canning room. No sooner were we inside than Lenny shouted again.

"Possum!" His voice was sharp. "What the heck's goin' on? Is somethin' wrong?"

We pulled the canning-room door most of the way closed, held our breath, and waited. Thirty more seconds went by, and then we heard Lenny again, his voice much closer.

"Possum, answer me, darn you! Stop screwin' around. Don't make me come down there! You ain't gonna like it if I do."

Another half minute went by, maybe more, and then we heard Lenny's footsteps as he descended the basement stairs. The boards squeaked on the third and then the seventh step, and then we heard his feet scuff the cement.

In the next second he must have seen the bloody trail leading into the other room, because he stopped. "What the . . ." he said softly.

I heard Possum let out a moan from the other room.

"Possum?" Lenny hissed, his voice full of caution.

After another second he stepped into our view. He had his back to us and held a flashlight in his left hand and a pistol in his right hand. He began to shine his light around the room where the coal bin was and he stepped through the door, following the blood.

I knew he must have spotted Possum, because I heard him say, "What happened to you?" as he hurried across the floor.

Possum was moaning louder now and trying to talk. "Gemme outta here. Gemme outta here," he mumbled. "There's ghosts."

It was time to move. I pulled the canning-room door open and gave Bee a nudge. She sprang out and tiptoed up the stairs, remembering to step over the two steps that squeaked. I hurried out after her, quickly reaching the top of the stairs and following her toward the kitchen.

As we came around the corner I was hoping we

could rescue the hostages right then. I couldn't hear Lenny behind us yet, so all we had to do was untie everyone, run outside, maybe jump in Grandma Em's car, and drive away. We would all go hide somewhere and wait for Judge Gator to show up with the police.

That idea lasted only until I got a good look at the prisoners. Grandma Em, Daddy, and the three LaBelles were each tied to a kitchen chair with thick rope that went around their arms, legs, and chests. I ran to the back of Daddy's chair, but the knots were pulled so tight, I couldn't budge them.

I needed a knife, and I cursed myself for leaving the X-acto on the workbench, but even with that I wouldn't have had enough time. I could already hear Lenny talking to Possum, his voice getting louder as they moved toward the basement stairs.

"Abbey," Daddy whispered. "Go! Don't let them catch you!"

Grandma Em hissed at Bee, who was pawing through a kitchen drawer looking for a knife. "Do what Mr. Force says. Get out now!"

I looked at Daddy and felt tears spring to my eyes because he was right. We had come so close, but we weren't going to free anyone, especially not if we were caught. And now Lenny would be here any second.

"Go!" Daddy hissed.

There were tears running down Bee's cheeks.

"Bee, get!" Grandma Em whispered.

Bee nodded blindly and turned toward the back door, but I grabbed her arm. "Not that way," I said. "We'll make too much noise."

I shoved her toward the hallway. "Go out the downstairs bathroom window."

The bathroom was just around the corner, a few steps down from the kitchen. Before we left, Bee turned.

"Donna," she whispered, "tell them you need to go to the bathroom."

Donna just blinked, too scared to even respond. There were stumbling sounds coming from the basement, which meant Lenny and Possum were starting to climb the stairs. We couldn't wait. I grabbed Bee's arm.

"Donna!" Bee whispered again. "Tell them you have to go to the bathroom! Understand?"

She stared at us, her eyes glazed and dull. More footsteps thumped on the stairs. Finally she nodded.

Once we were in the bathroom, I closed the door silently while Bee moved to the toilet, stood up on the seat, and grabbed the window. As she raised the sash, the sound of the storm rose sharply with the wind whistling through the joint where the two shutters came together. Together we undid the fastener and opened the shutters.

"Out quick," I whispered.

Bee was bigger than me, and the opening was small. Once she got her shoulders through, I picked up her feet to keep her from kicking and making noise and I shoved her the rest of the way. She thumped onto the ground below. This was followed by a groan and a muffled curse, but a second later she was on her feet waving me out.

Behind me in the hallway, very close, Possum let out a loud groan. "I'm tellin' ya," he said, his voice quavering with fear. "They was ghosts."

"Knock it off," Lenny said. "There ain't no such thing as ghosts. You musta knocked your head on somethin'."

I fought down a fresh wave of panic as someone grabbed the doorknob on the other side and started to give it a turn. The door was unlocked.

I climbed onto the toilet seat and stuck my head out the window, but I was too slow. The knob creaked. Lenny was going to grab me or shoot me before I got halfway out. Bee was reaching for my arms, ready to help pull me through, but it didn't matter because I wasn't going to make it.

Behind me the door squeaked as it started to open.

"Hey, Lenny," Daddy shouted, his voice very loud. "This young lady needs to go to the bathroom right now. Better let her go first, or you're going to have a big mess to clean up."

Daddy's shout gave me focus. He was thinking, even if I couldn't. It made me calm down and work my way forward. As I wriggled my hips through the window, the wind grabbed my hair and tore at my clothing. Raindrops smacked into me, soaking me at once. I welcomed the violence of the weather, knowing it meant freedom, even though any second hands could grab my ankles and pull me back inside.

Bee reached for my wrists and pulled me through the rest of the way, and we both splashed to the wet ground in a big lump. As soon as I hit I jumped back up, ignoring the pain.

"Quick," I whispered. "Get me on up your shoulders."

Bee squatted down, let me on, then struggled to her feet. From there I was able to reach up, grab the window sash, and slide it closed. I just had to hope so much rain hadn't splashed inside that it would give us away.

Bee let me down, and for a second we stood there collecting our wits. Part of me hoped we might have seen the flashing lights of police cars by now, but there was no sign of help. The storm continued to rage all around us, cutting us off from the world.

If the cavalry ever got here, Bee and I could quit what we were doing and let the police do the rescuing. But wishing wasn't going to save anybody. Daddy always said that when you're in a terrible storm, you have to assume that you and whoever you are with are the *only people in the world*, because for at least a few hours you may be that alone. At those times you have to think calmly and clearly and only worry about things you can actually do something about. That meant I couldn't worry about when the police would come.

I looked around and took a deep breath. While the rain was still very heavy, the wind was definitely dropping. Maybe the eye of the storm was approaching. It would mean the winds would become nearly dead calm and the sun might even come out for a brief time, but then the back side of the storm would hit us. While the winds would not be as strong as with the front edge, they would still be plenty bad.

Even as I was thinking these things, a faint sound came from inside the house. Donna LaBelle was looking out at us.

I got on Bee's shoulders again, and she staggered

over to the window, and I helped Donna raise the sash. Once it was up, I whispered, "Stick out your head and arms, and we'll pull you the rest of the way. Just be quiet."

She was standing on the toilet seat, but she looked so scared that I thought she might break into sobs. She just needed to keep quiet long enough to squirm out of the window without getting caught.

"I don't know if I can," she said in a too loud whisper.

I held my finger to my lips. "Stop it! You have to! Hurry up!"

She looked down at the ground and shook her head.

"Donna!" I said, in a voice sharp enough to make her eyes widen in surprise. "Don't you want to save your parents?"

She nodded, but she still looked frozen.

"You have to come out, right now! They're not going to let you alone for long. And if you go back in the kitchen, they're not going to let you live much longer." I reached out my hands. "Come on. Now!"

With the window open, the sounds from the house spilled out, and a fist hammered on the bathroom door. "Enough time. Come on out of there!" Lenny growled.

Donna looked over her shoulder; then she thrust out her hands and grabbed for mine. Behind her someone was shaking the bathroom door, but Donna must have locked it, because a second later a foot or shoulder slammed into it.

Donna squirmed out the window even as the lock broke and the door knocked back into the wall.

"Hey, come back here!" Lenny shouted.

I had Donna by the wrists and as she squirmed Bee backed up until Donna shot through and we all collapsed on the grass.

"Quick!" I whispered. I grabbed Donna and jerked her to her feet as the three of us ran behind the thick trunk of a nearby live oak. When I peeked back around the trunk, I could see Lenny looking out the window, swinging his head from side to side.

"Girl!" he roared. "You get back here right now, or I'm gonna hurt one'a your parents real bad. You hear me? Girl?"

Donna flinched beside me, and I grabbed her arm and held her in place. She'd been scared almost to death to start with and now that Lenny was threatening her parents she was even more scared, but if we were going to get all the prisoners out safe and in one piece, we needed her. She wasn't going to like the plan that was taking shape in my head, but it was the only plan we had.

Lenny yelled a few more times, but then he reached out, pulled the shutter closed, and fastened it. A second later the window slammed.

"We have to move!" I said. "They'll be coming after us any second."

We turned and started to run up the drive, away from the house. Behind us the front door of the big house banged open. It was still raining but not quite as hard as before. Lenny would be able to see us, and if he did, he'd probably start shooting.

There were fenced grassy pastures on our left, several barns and equipment sheds on our right, and behind them about fifty yards of woods and then a big field of collard greens, where we could get down on our bellies, crawl between the rows, and stay out of sight until we got to the much bigger woods on the other side.

"Over here," I said, heading in that direction. I vaulted the fence and Bee did the same thing. Donna slowed down and climbed over like an old person.

"Come on!" I shouted. Lenny was running in our direction, only about fifty yards behind.

Donna hopped off the fence and started to run. I

grabbed her arm and shoved her in front of me so I could make sure she kept moving. "Don't stop!" I commanded.

Behind us Lenny yelled something I could barely make out.

"But my parents—" Donna began.

"We're the witnesses. They can't hurt them unless they catch us," I shouted, hoping desperately that I was right, but knowing at the same time that surrender was not an option. "Run!"

Nineteen

Bee led the way toward the nearest equipment shed. She ran inside, past a couple of tractors and straight out the back. Donna followed and I came last. As I ran out the rear of the shed, I looked down, my eyes drawn instinctively to a black shape at my feet.

I almost screamed but realized instantly that the snake was too skinny and too long to be a cottonmouth. It was a black racer, a type of snake we protected because it was a great rodent eater.

Even though I knew Lenny was close behind, I stopped. A black racer is as fast as greased lightning and almost impossible to catch with your bare hands. When I looked more closely, I saw a cedar shingle that the wind had torn off one of the roofs. It had hit the snake right behind its head and killed it.

With a crazy idea lighting up in my head, I grabbed up the snake and ran after Bee and Donna. The snake hadn't been dead long. Its muscles were still loose, and it coiled naturally around my arm. Up ahead Bee and Donna had come to a barbed-wire fence and didn't know how to cross it. Bee saw the snake, but she was smart enough not to ask. Donna was looking in all directions, still too close to panic to notice.

"That way," I said, pointing. I knew where there was an easy place to get under just ahead.

The wind had died enough so that I could hear Lenny cursing behind us as he splashed along the flooded ground. He had almost reached the equipment shed, and I knew we had to hurry. If we could make it through the fence without him seeing how we did it, we might be in the clear.

We ran a few more yards, to a spot where the ground dipped into an indentation, so the lowest strand of barbed wire was a foot or two off the ground. The dip was filled with water, but Bee had already figured it out. She dove onto her belly and rolled through the water. For a second she completely disappeared but then came up on the other side of the wire and got to her feet.

Donna hesitated for a second, but then she got flat on her stomach and rolled into the water and out the other side.

Lenny was in the shed, checking behind the tractors and mowing attachments to make sure we weren't hiding. "You in here, girls?" he shouted.

I threw myself down as soon as Donna was out of my way and rolled into the water and out the other side. Once I was on my feet, I tucked the arm with the dead snake under my T-shirt and followed Bee and Donna into the swath of trees that stood behind the sheds. We quickly hid ourselves behind the ancient live oaks and tangles of wild grapes and thick wrists of honeysuckle that grew in tight profusion.

Right where we squatted a small hole in the undergrowth allowed us to peek back and see the equipment shed and part of the fence line. I could just make out Lenny. He was standing outside the back door, confused.

After a few seconds he balled his hands into fists. "I'm gonna start killin' your parents. You don't get back to the house right now, the first one dies in five minutes." He held up one arm that I guessed held his wristwatch. "I'm counting!"

Donna let out a moan. I took a deep breath and did a gut check. I *really, really* believed that Lenny wouldn't take the risk of killing four people if he knew he had three witnesses running around in the woods. If I was wrong, I would never be able to live with the consequences, but if I was right, we had no other choice than what we were about to do.

"Donna," I said. She had mud, sticks, and leaves in her normally perfect blond hair, and a big smear of dirt along one side of her face. Her clothes were soaked, torn, and filthy; her eyes bloodshot. She looked perfect for what we needed.

"Donna," I repeated. "You were right before. You have to go back. It's very important."

"Me?" Her eyes grew huge, and once again tears started to spill down her cheeks.

"You need to go back inside the house."

"Just me?" She looked at me like I had just threatened to cut off her arm. After a second she began to shake her head in tiny little movements that made me wonder if she was having a fit. "Sneak in?" she squeaked.

"No. You're going to go in the front door and let Lenny and Possum know you're back. You have to scare them, so I want you to start out by screaming."

"Why?"

"Because when you run into the house they need

to think you're running away from something really scary."

Donna gave me one of her looks. "I'm not going to start screaming."

"You have to. Do it now."

She rolled her eyes to tell me what an idiot I was; then she let out a scream that wouldn't have frightened a mouse. "There."

"It has to be louder and a lot scarier."

"That's as scary as I can make it."

"Then I'm going to help you."

With that I pulled out my arm from under my shirt and held out the snake.

The scream Donna let loose could have shattered glass.

"Get away!" she shrieked.

I kept the snake close to Donna's face, moving my arm fast so she couldn't tell it was dead.

"Get away! Get away! Get away!" she screamed, the words separated by guttural howls that made it sound as if she were being ripped to pieces by some horrible monster.

I waited a few more seconds; then I pulled the snake away and threw it behind me.

"Okay, okay," I whispered. "Quiet."

Donna was sucking in huge, shuddering breaths, her eyes flooded with tears, snot running all over her lips and chin. She was an absolute wreck and looked so pathetic that for a few seconds I was swamped by a huge wave of guilt, but it lasted only until I saw that Donna's scream had worked.

Through the snarl of branches I could see that Lenny had come back out of the equipment shed again and was standing on the other side of the barbed-wire fence. His mouth was wide open, and he was waving his pistol around as if he feared that whatever horrible creature had just eaten Donna might suddenly burst out of the trees and try to eat him. After another second he started backing toward the shed, keeping his gun aimed at the trees until he disappeared through the door. I smiled.

"You did great," I told her.

Donna shook her head. "You were going to let that snake bite me," she squeaked in a barely audible voice.

"The snake was dead. Besides, it's not even a poisonous snake."

Donna took that in, and for a second her fear seemed to fade and I caught a glint of anger in her eyes. "You tricked me?"

"Only to make you scream. We needed Lenny to hear you."

"Why?"

"Because it's important for when you go back to the house."

"I'm not doing it." She spoke with more force this time, and I actually felt a glimmer of hope that the old Donna was coming back.

"Yes, you are. It's the only way to make sure we get your parents and everyone else out safely."

"What are you talking about?"

"We'll explain it to you," Bee said.

It was everything I could do not to throw my arms around Bee and give her a big hug. We hadn't ever talked about this part of the plan, but she knew where I was going with it. In fact, knowing Bee, she was probably ahead of me.

Donna looked back and forth between us, then settled on Bee. "It's really the only way?" she asked.

"Yes."

"Come on," Bee said as I stood and started back toward the equipment shed. "We don't have much time. We'll explain it to you on the way."

Twenty

As we got back to the place where we would slide under the fence Donna stopped suddenly, stamped her foot, and spun around.

"You want me to say I'm being chased by ghosts? That's stupid!" she hissed. "They'll never believe me."

"Yes, they will," Bee insisted. "Possum thinks he's already seen a ghost."

"Why would he think that?"

"Because of the skull we used to scare him."

Donna looked even more skeptical. "Where did you guys get a skull?"

Bee and I exchanged a glance. I felt like we had to

tell her. "Donna," I began, "do you know why we're all in this mess?"

Donna's face twisted. She looked at Bee then back at me and shook her head.

"We're here and my father and Bee's grandmother are prisoners because your father was trying to break the law again."

"He is not!"

"I'm not sure what he's doing at Hangman's Bluff, but he ruined an old graveyard where slaves were buried a long time ago. That's against the law, for sure."

She swung her arm, pointing in the direction of the big house. "My parents are prisoners of those same crazy men, and you're talking about graves! Who cares about some old slave graves?"

Bee moved so fast, I never even saw it. She grabbed Donna by the shoulders and spun her around. Bee was so angry, her face looked like it belonged to a person I didn't know.

"My relatives were buried in those graves before your father wrecked them. *I* care, and I care a lot!"

There was fresh fear in Donna's eyes. She knew she'd made a huge mistake. Up to now she'd thought I was crazy and mean but that Bee was the one she might be able to count on for pity. Now Bee was mad enough to pound her into the ground like a tent stake.

"I . . . I didn't know," Donna said, all the fight seeping out of her.

"Well, your father *did* know! He knew it was wrong, but he didn't care. He just wanted to keep things quiet, so he hired some criminals to help him. And this is where it's gotten us."

Donna stumbled back a step or two and rubbed her shoulders where Bee's fingers had been digging in. She stared at the ground, the anger on her face replaced by a dull expression. "I'm sorry. I don't know what to say." She looked up. "What do you want me to do?"

"Come on," I said gently.

I rolled through the water and out the other side, then I signaled for Bee and Donna to wait while I crept to the doorway of the equipment shed and peeked around the corner, making sure Lenny wasn't inside waiting to surprise us. When I was sure the coast was clear, I waved for Bee and Donna.

"Okay," I said to Donna. "You are going to run into the house, and you're going to scream just as hard as you screamed when I held that snake in your face."

"How's that going to help?"

"We need to get Lenny and Possum out of the house. Can you do it?"

"Maybe . . . I don't know . . ."

"You did a good job when you screamed," Bee said with an encouraging smile. "You're a great actress. You really got them scared, but we need you to do it again, okay?"

Donna looked at Bee and gave an uncertain nod.

We crept back toward the house, looking around to make sure Lenny had gone back inside. Then, while Donna acted as a lookout on the front door, Bee and I picked up the picnic table that sat under a live oak in the backyard and moved it under the bathroom window.

My heart was in my mouth, because if Donna did her job well, I was going to have my part to play next, and that would mean keeping Possum and Lenny outside. Even though I tried not to let it show, I was scared halfway into next year. I crossed my fingers and toes and made a wish that it was all going to work. In the back of my mind, a voice was telling me that wishing wasn't going to make a single bit of difference. I was betting all our lives over what was about to happen next.

The wind still had teeth, but the rain had let up a tiny bit, falling in huge drops instead of sheets. I checked to make sure Bee was in position then ran back around to the front of the house, where Donna was waiting. She looked as scared as I felt.

"Ready?" I asked.

Donna swallowed hard and mouthed, *Okay.*

"On my signal."

I almost felt sorry for her as she turned and started toward the front door. Almost. I ran to the far side of the porch and unspooled the hose from its reel; then, holding one end, I ran back to the other side of the porch and hid in a thick grouping of azalea bushes.

Donna was shaking with fear as she tiptoed up the steps toward the front door, but then she seemed to steady herself. She took a deep breath, balled her hands into fists, shoved the door open, and began to scream like someone absolutely hysterical with fear.

I knew how scared I would have felt if I'd been going back into a house where Lenny and Possum were holding a bunch of people prisoner, so I have to admit I was pretty impressed with Donna's acting. She hollered the word, "Ghosts!" followed by a bunch of screams. Then she turned, ran off the porch and onto the gravel drive, and kept screaming.

Right away everything broke loose inside the house. Lenny and Possum shouted, their feet clomping on floorboards. A second later Possum came barreling out with his shotgun in one hand. He bounded down the porch steps, aiming for the plantation drive and the way off Reward. He never saw the hose when I jerked it tight, and he went smacking down on his face in the mud and standing water, his shotgun skidding away from him.

Lenny had followed him out onto the porch, and he was staring down at Possum in amazement. I knew that any second he was going to spot the hose and realize they were being tricked, but Donna must have understood it too, because right then she did something else that impressed me.

She actually ran back up onto the porch, right toward Lenny, still screaming her head off. He grabbed for her, but she just dodged him and hollered even louder.

By that time Possum had gotten onto his feet and started to run away from the house. Lenny stopped trying to catch Donna and shouted at Possum, "Come back here, you stupid fool. There ain't no such things as ghosts."

Once Lenny had turned away from her, Donna raced into the house, still screaming. I smiled, because she was doing her part perfectly. Right then she was heading toward the bathroom to unfasten the shutter, raise the window, and let Bee inside.

Possum's brain was fried. Not paying any attention to Lenny, he kept on running, not exactly sprinting but not walking, either. As his silhouette grew faint in the mist and rain, I darted out from the bushes.

Lenny might have missed seeing the hose, but he didn't miss seeing me as I jumped out from my hiding place, reached down in the mud, and picked up Possum's shotgun. My hands were trembling like oak leaves in the wind. I didn't know if the shells were soaked or if there was mud in the barrel, but I couldn't worry about that, because I couldn't let Lenny go back inside.

"You put down that gun, girl," he growled as he came off the porch, moving slow and cautious like he suspected we were springing some kind of trap on him.

"Drop your gun, mister," I said, trying hard to keep my voice from shaking as I pushed off the safety and aimed the shotgun at Lenny's midsection.

He looked at me for a second then let out an ugly laugh and shook his head. Instead of dropping his pistol, he brought it up to his hip so it was aiming at me. "That was you in the basement, wasn't it?"

I nodded. "Drop the gun." I sounded just as scared as I felt.

"You don't even know how to shoot that thing, girlie."

Lenny's cockiness gave me a welcome surge of

anger. "My daddy taught me to shoot well enough that I won't miss someone as fat as you, not at this range."

Lenny's eyes narrowed. "Maybe so, but you ain't gonna pull that trigger." He edged a step closer, and I took a step back.

"You stay right there," I said. "Or I really will shoot. I swear it."

My heart was slamming so hard in my chest that I could barely keep my eyes locked on Lenny. He was calling my bluff, and we both knew it. Even if he came right up to me and tried to take the gun away, I didn't know if I could shoot him. But then I thought about Daddy and Grandma Em and decided maybe I could, after all.

Lenny must not have been totally convinced, either, because he came another step toward me then stopped again. His face twitched as he thought about his odds. Time stretched. The gun was growing heavy in my hands. I thought about Bee and Donna. *Please hurry*, I said to them in my head.

Finally, Lenny took another step.

"Stay where you are!" I said.

He took another step. That's when I flicked the safety back on, because I already knew what was going to happen next.

A cast-iron frying pan hit Lenny in the back of the

head, swung by my very angry father. The pan made a wet sound as it connected, and Lenny dropped like a sack of dog food, landing on his face in a puddle.

Daddy kicked the pistol away, then rolled Lenny over so he didn't drown. Grandma Em came down the steps behind Daddy, followed by Bee. Grandma Em picked up Lenny's pistol and aimed it at him for good measure as Daddy came over, took the shotgun out of my trembling hands, and put his arms around me.

"You okay?" he asked.

I was shaking hard, partly from the fear I'd been feeling just a few seconds earlier and partly from relief. I could barely speak. "Yes," I managed, after a few seconds.

"That's my girl."

He straightened his arms and held me away from him as he looked at me for a long moment. I wasn't sure whether there were tears in his eyes or raindrops. "I don't know whether to spank you or kiss you," he said. "I'm proud of your bravery, but it just about kills me when you pull stunts like this."

I didn't get a chance to reply, because at that moment there were flashing lights behind me. It was the police, coming up the plantation drive. Two state police cars skidded to a stop, with Judge Gator's old Mercedes right behind. The policemen got out with their guns drawn, and Judge Gator jumped out as well.

"Thank heavens!" the judge exclaimed, when he saw me standing there with Daddy, and Bee standing beside Grandma Em. "You girls scared me half to death. I just got back to my house a little while ago and found your note." He shook his head as he looked down at Lenny. "But it looks like y'all managed pretty well on your own."

It took only about a minute for the police to get Lenny in handcuffs and hoist him back on his feet. He had a cut on the back of his head, but one of the policemen wiped it with some disinfectant from his first-aid kit then took a kitchen towel from the big house and tied it around Lenny's head.

While he did that, another officer went inside and got Leaper. They led the dog out of the house using a long stick with a loop at the end that went over his neck, just in case he got mean. Unlike when I'd seen him earlier with Possum, Leaper didn't look like he had a mean bone in his body. He sort of staggered as he walked, and when they opened up the back of one of the police cars, he got inside and went right to sleep.

A minute later they loaded Lenny into the backseat of a second cruiser, and seconds after that a third police car came up the drive with Possum in the backseat. The policeman who seemed to be in charge went over to the police car, opened the back door, and waved for Bee and me to come over.

"Is this the other man?" he asked.

"Yessir," we both said at the same time. I almost felt sorry for Possum, because, sitting there in handcuffs, he looked so bewildered and confused, like he couldn't quite understand all the terrible things that had happened to him over the past hour or so.

After another minute two of the police officers brought Donna and her parents out of the house. Mr. LaBelle was rubbing his wrists. The moment he spotted me, he came up and got right in my face.

"I can't believe you sent my daughter back into the house with those two men! What were you thinking? How dare you risk her life like that!"

I took a breath, but before I could get a word out, Donna stepped in front of me.

"It was the only way we could get the two of them out of the house. And by the way, Abbey was the one who stayed outside with Lenny and his gun while we cut you free!"

I was speechless. Donna was facing off against her father with so much ferocity that she reminded me of a mother wolf protecting her cub.

Daddy had overheard Mr. LaBelle's angry words, and now he stepped over as well. "What's the problem here?"

Mr. LaBelle looked from Donna to Daddy, and some of his confidence seemed to leak out. "Your daughter forced my daughter to go back inside the house," he said in a quieter tone. "It put her at serious risk."

"*Nobody* forced me!" Donna shouted.

Daddy's eyes got small. He didn't get angry very often, and I hadn't seen him like this since before his coma. When he spoke, his voice was soft and danger-ous.

"Bee and Abbey had the courage to sneak into that house and get your daughter out in the first place. Then Abbey had the guts to face down a killer with a loaded pistol in his hand while Donna and Bee cut us loose. What they did allowed us all to get out of there alive. If you say one more thing to her, you will be speaking through broken teeth."

Mr. LaBelle opened his mouth, then closed it. He took a step back, and his lip curled. "My lawyer will be in touch."

Daddy was about ready to take a swing at Mr. LaBelle, but then the sound of a deep voice broke in.

"Mr. LaBelle, you mind if I ask you a few questions?"

I turned and saw Deputy Cyrus Middleton standing a few feet away and realized that he must have driven up while we were all focused on Mr. LaBelle.

Mr. LaBelle barely glanced toward Deputy Middleton. "I think the questions can wait," he said in a snippy voice. "We've all gone through quite a harrowing experience."

"Actually, sir, they can't."

Twenty-one

As we watched Deputy Middleton's car disappear down the drive with the LaBelles inside Bee turned to look at the rest of us. "We have to go to Hangman's Bluff."

"Why?" I asked.

Bee had a gleam in her eye.

"We have to get Yemassee," I remembered.

"She's really there?" Judge Gator asked, his voice trembling. "And she's okay? And the puppies?"

Bee and I nodded.

"Well, let's go!"

Twenty minutes later the sky overhead had turned

to blue haze and the storm was a dark smudge in the northwest as Bee, Grandma Em, Judge Gator, Daddy, and I piled out of Judge Gator's old Mercedes at Hangman's Bluff. Mr. and Mrs. LaBelle and Donna and Deputy Middleton were there as well; I guess the deputy had insisted on getting some answers right then and there. Two other state police cars had come along with him.

At that moment Mr. LaBelle had his hands on his hips like a teacher who was put out with a dumb student. "My family has been through enough," he snapped at the deputy. "I can't believe you are subjecting us to this harassment."

Deputy Middleton nodded, but he didn't back down. "Sir, are you the owner of this parcel of land known as Hangman's Bluff?" He spoke in that deep voice where the words came so slow that they reminded me of molasses being poured out of a bottle. If a person only listened to the words, they might think Deputy Middleton wasn't the sharpest knife in the drawer. But if a person watched the deputy's eyes, they would never make that mistake. I noticed that Mr. LaBelle was barely looking at him.

"You know I am," Mr. LaBelle said.

"And you had hired the two suspects we just apprehended?"

"Yes, they worked for me, but I had no idea about any crimes they may have committed."

"And what were you paying them to do?"

I realized that Bee had edged very close to my shoulder and gone so still that she reminded me of a dog holding point on a covey of quail. Right then I knew Bee was listening harder than all the rest of us put together, and that if Mr. LaBelle told a lie, she was going to sense it right away.

Mr. LaBelle rolled his eyes and sighed. "They were excavating topsoil because I've been selling it. As you know I've owned Hangman's Bluff for years." Here he turned his head and gave Daddy a dirty look. "Since the land isn't worth anything near what I paid for it, I've been trying to think of ways to recoup a portion of my investment. Selling the topsoil was one way."

I caught a flicker of something in Deputy Middleton's dark eyes, but I was pretty sure Mr. LaBelle missed that, too. He was way too busy being offended at having to answer these questions.

"How much topsoil you reckon you have on that land, sir?" Deputy Middleton asked.

"I don't know!" Mr. LaBelle snapped. "Do I look like I've been running the backhoe?"

Deputy Middleton seemed to take no offense. "No, sir, but I'm curious just the same. How much topsoil? How deep does it go?"

Mr. LaBelle shook his head. "Maybe a couple feet?" he said, making it more of a question than an answer.

Deputy Middleton nodded his huge head. "We do have some of the best topsoil anywhere on these river islands."

"Yes, now are we done here?" Mr. LaBelle shot back.

Deputy Middleton didn't appear to have heard the question. "So how come you been having your men dig so deep?" he persisted. "Judging by this hole here, you musta dug down another six feet at least. Did you find somebody someplace who wants to buy all that fill? It's just marl and clay under the topsoil. Had to be real expensive to truck it out of here."

I saw a pinched look come into Mr. LaBelle's eyes, like maybe he didn't like where all these questions were heading. "So, maybe it was," he said. "Do we really have to waste time talking about my business decisions?"

"I'm just curious why you'd do that. Seems like a money loser."

"Losing money on a bad deal isn't a crime, is it?"

Deputy Middleton didn't appear to have heard him. "Did you find anything interesting in all that dirt?"

By now the tension of the whole group had gone

way up. The other policemen seemed to be hanging on the answers to Deputy Middleton's questions. Bee's shoulder was touching mine, and I felt her trembling, with barely controlled anger.

Mr. LaBelle shook his head. "Nope."

"Liar!" Bee exploded.

Mr. LaBelle swung his eyes toward her, his face pale with anger. "How dare you, young lady, I—"

Bee paid him no attention. "You found an old slave graveyard," she snapped. "But you didn't want to stop your digging, so you didn't report it. You just treated the bones like they were a bunch of old garbage."

Mr. LaBelle shot a glance at the policemen. "I . . . I don't know anything about that," he said.

Grandma Em had moved over to stand right beside Bee and put an arm around her shoulder. Still, she didn't try to shush her.

"I don't believe you," Bee said in a much quieter voice. "The whole reason the judge's dog got stolen was because she had found something that day that Lenny and Possum dug up. It was a human bone, wasn't it? And Yemassee was bringing it home. Lenny and Possum knew that if Yemassee's owner recognized the bone as human, and if he somehow traced it back here, that you'd all be in big trouble, so Lenny went to get the bone back. You just didn't expect Lenny to steal the dog, did you?"

My jaw was on the floor. Of course that's what Yemassee had been carrying. Bee had figured it out—and faster than me, no surprise.

Mr. LaBelle wrinkled his face as if that was totally ridiculous. "I didn't know anything about the bones or the stolen dog or about any of the other things those men did."

I cleared my throat. "Why did you put in an old rice gate?"

The policemen all turned to look at me, and their eyebrows went up. Mr. LaBelle looked at them, then at me, and seemed to take a moment to think about his answer. "Okay, I'll admit I had another plan with this land. I was waiting for a big storm to breach that rice gate. When the hole flooded naturally, I thought I could make it into a marina for the boats. And with the land essentially underwater, nobody on the island could stop me."

Mr. LaBelle closed his eyes and shook his head. "I never meant for anybody to get hurt," he said, after a moment. "I know it was wrong, but I just wanted to get back some of the money I'd lost."

He raised his head and gazed toward where Mrs.

LaBelle and Donna were standing a few feet away. "I'm just so sorry to cause my family more heartache."

Deputy Middleton asked a few more questions, but after everything we'd been through, everyone seemed pretty exhausted. The small group of us stood around as if we didn't know quite what to say or what to do next. Judge Gator broke the silence by asking, "Where's Yemassee?"

Bee and I pointed at the construction trailer, and the judge started walking fast through the mud toward it. I was getting ready to follow, but I didn't move right away. I found myself actually feeling a little sorry for Mr. LaBelle. He had done a really bad thing, digging a hole and waiting for a storm to fill it in so he could have a marina and try to get around all the zoning laws . . . again. But I actually thought he might have learned his lesson this time, since it had almost cost him his life along with the lives of his wife and daughter.

The rain had stopped completely, and the air was cool. Daddy had his arm around my shoulder, and Grandma Em had her arms around Bee. It reminded me of one of those happily-ever-after movie endings, with everyone smiling and the sun coming out just as all the bad guys have been beaten.

I was feeling about as tired as I've ever felt, but also

good. Bee and I had faced down a couple of really bad men, and also saved a bunch of other people *and* we had found the old slave graves and Yemassee. I didn't think there were a lot of twelve-year-old girls who could've done all that. Force & Force Investigations had really come through. I have to admit that I was feeling a little cocky right about then.

All those prideful feelings changed when I swung my gaze over to Daddy and noticed the dark bags under his eyes. Grandma Em's eyes looked the same, and it reminded me that Bee and I had done something good, but before that we had done something really, really stupid. Kayaking up to Hangman's Bluff right in front of a major storm when we should have been home helping Daddy and Grandma Em had been dangerous and irresponsible and selfish and cruel.

I flashed back to how I had felt a year earlier when Daddy had been in a coma and I thought I had lost the last person in the world who I really cared about. I remembered how horrible and alone I felt then, and Bee and I had just put the people we loved the most through those same horrible feelings.

That's when I started to cry. It wasn't any secret that I *hated* crybabies, so when I started sobbing, Daddy looked at me in alarm. "What's the matter?" he asked.

I threw my arms around him and just stood there sobbing. When I could finally get enough of a breath to talk, I managed to say, "I'm so sorry."

By that point Bee was crying, too, because she realized exactly why I was crying, and because kayaking to Hangman's Bluff had been her idea in the first place, she felt even worse than me about what we had done. Probably Daddy and Grandma Em had felt like spanking both of us before all the tears started, but they both seemed to feel sorry for how incredibly bad we felt, and they hugged us and gradually got us calmed down and cheered up a little.

Judge Gator cheered us up when he called down to us from the construction shed and got everyone's attention. "Come on up here. I got a little surprise for y'all."

I turned away from Daddy's tear-stained chest, and all of us walked toward where Judge Gator stood in the open door of the double-wide.

"In all this craziness, you girls managed to find my dog," he said with tears in his eyes and his voice hoarse with emotion. "I don't know how I can ever thank you enough."

Bee and I looked past him at where Yemassee lay on the floor, wagging her tail with five little balls of fur bunched around her tummy.

Seeing them made me feel like the sun had finally come out again, because even though I knew Bee and I were about to get the worst punishment of our lives, I was so happy that Judge Gator finally had his family back.

That afternoon Bee and I helped Daddy and Grandma Em open shutters and clean things up around Reward. We still didn't have power that night, so Daddy went down to the freezer and pulled out a couple of venison backstraps that he defrosted and then broiled on the grill in the backyard. He also got our generator and Grandma Em's generator running, so we had enough electricity to keep the lights on, and we invited Grandma Em and Bee and Judge Gator over for an early dinner.

The sky was perfectly clear, and the clouds from the storm had totally disappeared up the coast, leaving us with a beautiful sunset and a light, cool breeze. Even the mosquitoes and gnats had been blown away by the storm.

Both houses had come through without any damage, and with the shutters open once again the slanted evening light flowed in through the windows.

Outside the grill was smoking in a yard that was

littered with tons of leaves and blown-down limbs. It was going to take days to get all that stuff cleared away. Rufus was wandering around, sniffing all the strange new things. When Bee and I wandered out on the porch, I could see that the side of the house was still plastered with wet leaves that had been blown hard against the clapboards by the hurricane.

Everybody was happy to be together, but we were quiet and thoughtful and totally exhausted from all the things that had happened that day. After we ate, Daddy brought a watermelon onto the porch and cut it into pieces, and everybody sat and enjoyed the first truly cool evening of the season.

Judge Gator and Daddy had spoken further to the police, who had told them that Lenny and Possum were ex-cons who had done time in the state penitentiary for armed robbery. The police also said that just like seasoned criminals neither one of them had said a word other than to insist that the whole situation had been the result of a dispute caused by Mr. LaBelle refusing to pay them for all the work they had done. They also claimed that Mr. LaBelle had been the one who insisted on not reporting the grave sites. So far they had both been charged with home invasion, which would put them back in prison for sure, but the police were waiting for ballistics tests to come back on Lenny's gun, because they suspected it had been used to kill the man named Jimbo.

Bee and I tried to keep listening to what the judge was saying, but I caught Bee yawning a couple times. As for me, I could barely keep my own eyes open. I was dead tired and needed to go to bed before I fell asleep in my chair.

Just when I thought the talk was finally dying down and I was about to excuse myself, Daddy sat forward in his chair and shook his head. "I still don't understand why Lenny and Possum were prepared to kill people. What were they hoping to achieve?"

Judge Gator shrugged. "They're not very bright. They probably figured they'd go back to prison for desecrating the graves."

"Even so, they wouldn't have gotten more than a few months. You think those stakes are high enough to commit murder?"

Grandma Em nodded. "For Lenny I think they were. I'm not so sure about Possum."

Judge Gator scowled. "I agree with you, Em. If I were still on the bench and the jury found that bum guilty, I'd want to put Lenny in a cell and weld the door shut."

I had been slumped in my chair, only halfway listening. Even so, something had been bothering me, but I hadn't been able to put my finger on it. But what the judge said sent a charge through my body. I sat up, and my tiredness fell away.

"*Weld* the door shut," I repeated. I was suddenly picturing the two dirt piles and the hollowed-out places where we had hidden when we were trying to get away from Possum and Leaper. I looked over at Bee, who just a few seconds earlier had been about to fall asleep like me but who suddenly looked wide-awake.

"You remember that mask I threw?" I asked, even though I could tell she was thinking the exact same thing as me.

Bee nodded. "I was too scared to focus on it when we were hiding, but now I'm remembering that stuff we saw."

"Those tanks?"

Bee turned to Daddy. "What kind of gas was on that truck that got stolen?"

Daddy's brow wrinkled like he wasn't sure why she was asking, but he said, "It's called acetylene. It's used for welding."

"Remember all those hunks of metal on the ground in the second place we hid?" Bee said to me.

"Yeah."

"Can't a person use a welding torch to cut metal?"

"Yes," Daddy said.

"They weren't going to kill us because of the graves," Bee said, and we both jumped to our feet.

I remembered what Possum had said. *They been lookin' around.* At the time I'd thought he'd been talking about the bones, but I'd been wrong.

"We need to go to Hangman's Bluff," I said.

"That's ridiculous," Grandma Em said in a no-nonsense voice. "It's dark outside, and everyone is exhausted."

"No," Bee shot back. "Abbey's right. We need to go there, and we need to go right now!"

"What are you girls talking about?" Judge Gator demanded.

We don't have time to explain," I told him. "But call the police. We really need to hurry."

Twenty-two

We piled into Daddy's Suburban and headed toward Hangman's Bluff. Bee and I both refused to explain what we thought we'd find, because we were both afraid that nobody would believe us.

Judge Gator followed in his own car, but first he put in calls to Cyrus Middleton and the state police, explaining where we were going and asking them to meet us there.

When we took the turn toward Hangman's Bluff, Daddy had to go slow because of the huge puddles that had turned the dirt road to soup and the downed branches that nearly blocked our way in a few places.

Daddy's headlights lit up the road ahead, and there was what looked like a fresh set of tire tracks in the soft dirt. When we reached the end of the road, we found that the chain from the gate had been unlocked and left in the dirt.

"You think Cyrus could have gotten here ahead of us?" Daddy asked.

"Doesn't seem likely," Grandma Em said.

"I agree," Daddy said. He shut off his lights, and we crept forward using the soft glow of the moon to see our way. When we got up near the construction shed, I spotted the outline of a car up ahead, and Daddy stopped and turned off the Suburban's engine. We had the windows down, and in the sudden silence we could hear the growl of a bulldozer's engine.

Daddy said to be as quiet as if we were turkey hunting, meaning that instead of slamming doors, we pushed them until they touched the locks, then gave them a final harder nudge to click them closed.

As we were getting ready to check things out another darkened car came snaking toward us and Judge Gator climbed out. "Cyrus is on his way," he said. "So are the state police."

Daddy, Judge Gator, and Grandma Em led the

way as we walked toward the sound of the bulldozer. When we were about fifty yards away, Daddy held up his hand as a sign for us to stop, and we watched as the bulldozer shoved a bunch of dirt to close up one of the openings where Bee and I had hidden earlier that day.

It took only a couple minutes for the bulldozer operator to finish, and then he backed up the dozer and shut off the engine.

The silence fell in around us, the night being much quieter than normal since the frogs and crickets weren't singing the way they would have been if there hadn't been a storm.

The man started walking toward us, but he came to a sudden stop when he saw us standing there in the moonlight.

"Evening, Mr. LaBelle," Judge Gator said in a calm voice.

"Wha—? Judge DeSaussure? What are you doing out here?"

"I might ask you the same question."

"Who have you got with you? Why are you on my land? You're trespassing, you know."

"I've got Rutledge Force and Emma Force and the two girls. They apparently saw something earlier today that they didn't understand at the time, but it makes sense to them now."

I saw Mr. LaBelle's right hand drift down to his pants pocket, and I suddenly wondered if he had a gun in there. I was about to shout something to Daddy, but then I heard the unmistakable click of the judge's shotgun as he closed the chamber. In the dark I hadn't even noticed that he had it with him.

"You need to keep your hands away from your pockets," he said to Mr. LaBelle.

"This is an outrage!" Mr. LaBelle snapped. He was doing his best to sound angry and offended, but there was fear just beneath.

"What was so important that you had to run the bulldozer in the dark?" Daddy asked.

"That's none of your business."

I saw Mr. LaBelle's eyes go to either side, as if he was getting ready to make a run for it. It was pretty dark, even with the moon, and he might have had a decent chance of getting away. Only, right at that moment, three more cars came zooming up and stopped behind us. Their headlights lit the whole area like a football stadium during a night game.

Cyrus Middleton came walking right past us with a state police officer on either side of him. The officers all had their hands on their weapons, and it was pretty obvious that if Mr. LaBelle intended to run, he didn't have a chance.

"What are you doing here?" Mr. LaBelle demanded, still trying to pretend he was totally mystified. I had to give him credit for being a really good liar.

Before the officers could say anything, I spoke up. "He stole the gas truck and also the armored car. They're in the dirt piles."

"What are you talking about? Are you people listening to these . . . children?"

"They're in the dirt pile," Bee said. "We both saw them, but we didn't realize what they were. That's why Mr. LaBelle is here tonight. He was filling in those hollows so if the police came out here over the next few days, they wouldn't find them."

"That's ridiculous," Mr. LaBelle insisted. "I was a prisoner of those two criminals just like your parents!"

I shook my head. "Lenny said something about you wanting to throw him and Possum to the wolves. That saying has been bothering me all night, because I didn't understand what he was talking about, but now I do. Lenny realized you were going to double-cross them and claim they had been behind all this and that you were innocent. That was why they took you prisoner, wasn't it?"

Mr. LaBelle looked at me for a second, and then he just hung his head.

"Your own wife and daughter could have been killed," Bee said.

That was when Mr. LaBelle started to cry. "I couldn't let them think I was a criminal," he said in a choked voice.

"Even if it got all of you killed?" Bee asked.

"By then it was too late," he sobbed. "Lenny thought he could take all the money for himself if he got rid of us."

The policemen put the cuffs on Mr. LaBelle, and one of the policemen patted him down and took a pistol out of his pants pocket.

Mr. LaBelle didn't say another word.

As they led Mr. LaBelle past us to their car, Deputy Middleton stopped. "How did you figure all that out?"

"Well, after dinner Judge Gator said something about welding, and I remembered how we'd thrown a welding mask over that dirt mound to try to distract Possum."

Bee added, "It just kind of clicked for both of us at the same instant. We remembered the tanks we'd seen and the trucks and the thick pieces of metal."

One of the state policemen shook his head. "They

stole the acetylene so they could get rid of the armored car by cutting it into pieces?"

"Yes," I said. "Everybody thought they robbed the gas company to get money, but it was all about the acetylene."

Then Bee added, "And Mr. LaBelle was trucking lots and lots of dirt off the island. I bet if you find out where he dumped it, you'll find pieces of the armored car."

Deputy Middleton looked at us and nodded. "If it wasn't for you girls, he just might have gotten away with it."

As we drove home Bee and I were smiling. We were both as proud as we could be that we had figured everything out. The police had even found a box buried behind the double-wide with what looked like the missing eight million dollars. Bee and I were so delighted with ourselves that we forgot that we were supposed to get punished, and we asked Grandma Em and Daddy if we could have a sleepover. Apparently they were either so tired or so proud of us that they forgot, too, because they agreed.

We went straight to bed when we got home, but it was way too early the next morning when Daddy and

Grandma Em both showed up at my bedroom door and told us to get up right away and come down for breakfast, because there was something important we needed to do. I pulled the pillow over my head, thinking that the punishment I thought we had dodged the night before was awaiting us in the kitchen.

After a second I rolled over and looked at Bee in the other bed, who was looking just as sleepy as I felt. "What are they talking about?"

"No idea," she muttered.

We came down to the kitchen a few minutes later to find Daddy scrambling eggs. Buttered toast and crisp bacon was already on the table, which was a welcome sight, but I was still as nervous as a chicken in a meat factory.

Bee and I sat at the table, rubbed the sleep from our eyes, and waited for somebody to tell us what was going on. It was only after Daddy had spooned out the eggs and we all started to eat that they told us.

"What you girls did—and I'm talking about the *good* part, not the very, very *stupid* part—was incredibly brave," Grandma Em began. "But you know, it was not just the two of you who accomplished it."

I shot a sideways glance at Bee, who was already looking at me. We both smelled a really big rat.

"There was another girl involved," Grandma Em went on.

"Donna?" I said. I glanced at Daddy, but he had that stony look on his face that said he was 100 percent behind what Grandma Em was saying.

"While it was very difficult on all of us, it was hardest on her because of her father. While Mr. LaBelle may have done a lot of terrible things, I believe Donna still loves her father very much. His trial is going to be long and shameful and difficult, and it will be in the news every single day. I believe that you girls need to stand by Donna."

"Grandma!" Bee exclaimed. "You don't know her! She's horrible."

Grandma Em held up a hand for silence. "I know how you girls feel, but when people are in need, we do not worry about whether we like them. We worry about helping them."

I rolled my eyes, and Daddy caught it and said in a warning tone, "Abigail, are you listening?"

He'd called me Abigail. "Yessir," I muttered.

A knock on the kitchen door interrupted everything, and a second later Judge Gator walked in. "Almost ready?" he said.

It was then plain as day why Daddy and Grandma

Em had allowed us to have our sleepover. They were in cahoots along with Judge Gator and wanted us corralled up so we'd be easier to control.

"What do we have to do?" Bee asked.

"We're going over to see Donna and her mother," Grandma Em said. "I'm sure they had a very difficult night."

Twenty minutes later we pulled into a driveway in a suburb of small houses I hadn't been to before. We were in Daddy's Suburban with Judge Gator following behind, and when we pulled up to a single-level house on a quiet corner, we all climbed out and walked to the front door. Grandma Em had brought a baked ham, a basket of collards and tomatoes from her garden, and a bouquet of flowers. She and Daddy went first and rang the bell.

A second later Mrs. LaBelle came to the door. She was wearing a robe, her hair was a mess, and there were dark bags the size of ice-cream scoops under her eyes. She just stood there for a few seconds looking at all the things Grandma Em had brought, and right away I saw tears start to gather in the corners of her eyes.

She took the ham and the flowers and the basket of greens from Grandma Em, then turned around to try and mop her tears. As she did she called out to Donna. A few seconds later Donna appeared from somewhere in the back of the house, not looking any better than her mother. Bee and I knew what we had to do, and even though we weren't happy about it, we knew it was no use fighting Daddy and Grandma Em.

I took a step forward. "Bee and I thought you were really brave yesterday," I told her.

"Most kids our age could never have done what you did," Bee added. "You should be proud of yourself. You're also an awesome actress."

Donna looked back and forth between us. "Thanks," she said after a few seconds.

Donna's mom surprised me when she gave us a nice smile. "You and Bee were very brave, too," she said. "All of us owe you girls our thanks."

Judge Gator cleared his throat. "Would you girls please step over to my car?"

We all did as he asked, but when the judge spoke, he looked only at Donna. "Young lady," he said, "several days ago, my Boykin spaniel, Yemassee, was stolen right before she was due to have puppies." He glanced at Bee and me then turned back to Donna.

"Now, it appears that my dog has been found, and it also appears that all five of her puppies are in fine shape.

It's too soon for the puppies to leave their mother, but it might be fun to see them, don't you think?"

Without waiting for an answer, Judge Gator opened up the tailgate window and then dropped the bottom so we could all see Yemassee with her puppies in the back of the car. He reached in, picked up one of the puppies, looked it over, and held it out to me. "I've already talked to your dad and Grandma Em and gotten their blessings, and I believe this one ought to be yours," he said.

I was stunned. I already had been looking at that pup because he was the biggest dog in the litter. I took him and cradled him gently in my arms and smelled his wonderful puppy scent. He was calm, looking up at me and not wriggling all around. Daddy always said the early mark of a good hunting dog is one that pays attention to you and not his littermates. His eyes were barely open, but it felt incredible to think that in just a few weeks he might come home to live with Daddy, me, and Rufus.

The judge handed Bee a little girl puppy, saying, "I picked out a boy for Abbey, because I think she and her daddy would like a hunting dog, but I picked out a nice little girl for you."

Bee put out her arms and held her future puppy and

beamed at the judge. "Thank you," she said.

"It'll be six weeks at least before they should be taken from Yemassee," the judge said. "But after that she'll be yours to take care of and train. And if you ever decide you want her to hunt, I'll show you some things about training a good bird dog."

The judge turned and looked at Donna and her mom. "Now, there's just one more thing. Donna, why don't you look in there and see if there might be a puppy you'd like to have."

Donna's eyes went wide with surprise, and she walked over to look in at the remaining puppies. She stood there for a moment, eyeing them; then she pointed to the smallest one. The judge reached back inside the car and came out with it.

"In almost every litter there is a small, special puppy that we call the runt. Runts normally don't become great hunting dogs, but they make wonderful, loving pets. Now, I'm guessing you and your mother aren't avid hunters. Is that correct?"

Donna was staring at the judge with amazement and hope and maybe even a little bit of happiness in her eyes. She nodded. "Yessir," she said in a quiet voice.

"Well, since what you did was just as brave as what Abbey and Bee did, I want you to have that puppy. Do you think you and your mother could give this little girl a home?"

Donna looked up at her mother, who smiled and nodded.

The judge put the smallest Boykin into Donna's arms, and I swore I could actually see something warm and friendly come alive in her eyes. It almost made me think there might be some hope for her yet.

Twenty-three

The reason the big hole at Hangman's Bluff never flooded was thanks to Deputy Middleton's quick thinking. When he went to check the rice gate, he realized it was just about to give way, so he started up the bulldozer, drove it down into the hole, and pushed a bunch of marl up against it. The marl was heavy and full of clay, and it kept the old wood from giving way under the force of the river.

Because the hole didn't flood completely, it meant the bones from the broken graves weren't washed away and lost, and the police gave Professor Washburn permission to gather them up and move them to a different place. Over the next week, Bee and I rode our ponies over several times to watch Professor Washburn and his team of archeology students from the College of Charleston as they carefully sifted through the mud and dirt for more remains. In their digging they had identified the bones of at least twenty-five people.

The police were also digging, but but not for bones. Out of one of the big dirt piles, they unearthed the stolen gas truck and a whole bunch of silver tanks that said Old South Bottled Gas. In the other pile, they found what was left of the armored car. It looked like our hunch was right, and that Lenny and Possum had been using the welding gear and the stolen gas to cut up the armored car into pieces that they hauled away with all the marl Mr. LaBelle was trucking off the island.

The last day we were there was after school on Friday. That morning Bee and I had presented the joint project that we had done for our history assignment. It was titled "How the History Sisters Came to Be: The Story of Two Families."

The report started:

Our families came together nearly three hundred years ago. A rice planter headed one family. He had come to this country from France to find religious freedom and seek his fortune.

He bought a plantation on Leadenwah Island and named it Reward.

We don't know much about the other family. We don't know how old they were, how many children they had, or even their names, because they had been imprisoned and brought here from Africa. They did not speak the language or share the culture or religion of the planter family. They were slaves, and coming to the plantation was anything but a reward for them.

Our report examines what happened over these three hundred years, to acknowledge the wrongs and the suffering but also to recognize that, in some cases, quite by accident, unbreakable bonds were formed, bonds that are very much like traditional family ties between blood relatives. We aren't trying to say that those bonds in any way justify what came before; only that sometimes, very unexpectedly, very good things can come from very bad things. We believe that is a reason for us to try to practice forgiveness and to have hope for our futures.

We got an A+, thanks to the fact that Bee wrote most of it.

That afternoon Bee and I were both still tired

out from the craziness of the past week and the work involved in writing our paper, so we were moving slowly. By the time we finally got to Hangman's Bluff, all of Professor Washburn's student diggers had quit for the day, and the place was deserted.

The big piles of dirt were still where they had been, but the trucks and tanks of gas had been taken away. Strips of orange tape that said POLICE CRIME SCENE NO TRESPASSING fluttered in the wind.

We ignored the tape, tied up our ponies, and walked over to the edge of the huge hole that Mr. LaBelle had dug into what had once been beautiful old farmland. Even though the students were gone, we could see where they had driven wooden stakes into the ground and broken up the entire area into squares lined out with white string.

Down below us were the tools the archeologists used. There was a long wooden table, a group of large shovels and small hand trowels, and brushes and boxes with mesh screening on their bottoms. The boxes were used to sift through the loose dirt to trap bones, or perhaps coins or shards of pottery that had been buried with the dead slaves to help them in their journey to wherever their spirits were headed.

Out beyond the trenched ground, the lowering sun

glinted hard off the Leadenwah River, forcing us to shield our eyes. A steady wind blew off the water, and the humid, warm air brought with it the familiar scents of pluff mud, shellfish beds, and the distant ocean.

Bee seemed to be lost in thought as she stared out at the river with a faraway look in her eyes, but after a few seconds she sensed me watching her.

"Can you hear it?" she asked.

"Hear what?"

"The spirits, the ones Mrs. Middleton was talking about. I don't think they're angry any longer."

"Bee, there's no way—"

She held up a hand, shushing me. We stood there with the sun dying slowly in the west and the breeze ruffling our hair. At first the only sound I heard was the splash of a distant mullet and the low whistle of wind as it whispered through the marsh grass. But then, after a few seconds, I heard something else. Singing.

The sound was so low and so soft that I really couldn't be certain, but up from the ground all around us came what sounded like low voices raised in some kind of gospel song.

When I glanced at Bee again, I saw that a tear had broken loose from her eye and was trickling down her cheek. She made no move to wipe it away.

"You hear it?" she whispered.

As I nodded I was thinking about families, all kinds of families—about my family and Bee's family, not just now but going back over the centuries. I thought about all the wrongs and all the pain that had been inflicted by my family onto hers. I thought about how neither Bee nor I could do anything to change what had come before, but if we could remember that we were bound together not only by our common past but also by our friendship, we could take that whole ugly stew of history and make something good from it. Heck, who knew for sure, but maybe we could even make that same idea work where Donna LaBelle was concerned. Maybe.

I put my arm around Bee's shoulder and gave her a hug. A minute later we turned around, the sun to our backs now, making our shadows huge, much bigger than we would ever be. We mounted our ponies and headed for home.

Acknowledgments

There are many people without whose help this book would never be what it is. I would like to thank John Rashford, professor of anthropology at the College of Charleston, for his patience and generosity in educating me on many aspects of slave graveyards and the burial customs of enslaved people. I would also like to thank Edward Bennett, Esq., for his friendship and his apparently inexhaustible willingness to guide me through the legal complexities touched on in my books. Thanks always to my wife, Julia, whose love, patience, and encouragement keep me on course, and to my daughter, Liza, for her willingness to read the early drafts and provide honest criticism. Thanks to Jordan Brown, my editor, without whose high standards and remorseless editing this book would have fallen far short, and to Kellie Celia and all the other folks too numerous to be named at HarperCollins/Walden Pond Press for their expertise and rigorous attention to so many details that help transform a pile of words into something truly special. Thanks to Brett Helquist for yet another amazing and evocative cover. And, as always, thanks to Stephen Barbara at Foundry Literary and Media, without whose tenacity, guidance and tireless support none of this could have happened.